THE SHOOTING SCRIPT
A MIDWINTER'S TALE

SCREENPLAY AND INTRODUCTION BY
KENNETH BRANAGH

A Newmarket Shooting Script Series Book

NEWMARKET PRESS • NEW YORK

For David Barron, Tim Harvey, Iona Price, Tamar Thomas, and Terry Pritchard

96 97 98 99 10 9 8 7 6 5 4 3 2 1

Library of Congress Cataloging-in-Publication Data
Branagh, Kenneth.
A midwinter's tale : the shooting script / by Kenneth Branagh.
p. cm. — (A Newmarket screenplay)
ISBN 1–55704–274–8
I. A midwinter's tale (Motion picture) II. Title.
PN1997.I477B7 1995
791.43'72—dc20

95-45331
CIP

Quantity Purchases

Companies, professional groups, clubs, and other organizations may qualify for special terms when ordering quantities of this title. For information, write Special Sales, Newmarket Press, 18 East 48th Street, New York, New York 10017, or call (212) 832-3575.

Book design by Tania Garcia
Manufactured in the United States of America.

First Edition

CONTENTS

INTRODUCTION

"**C**omedy is a very serious business," said David Garrick (among others). My experience in the theatre is that comedy also springs from very serious business. The more "serious" the play the more likely rehearsals are to create amusement, not always intentional, not always enjoyed by the people involved. In Shakespeare particularly, the great tragedies tread such a fine line between laughter and tears, that any group working on them can find themselves in the grip of hysteria. Especially if, as is often the case, time is short. It means that relationships between actors, directors, stage managers, designers—the ad hoc "family" that is a theatrical company—become very intense. Angry showdowns, love affairs, nervous collapses, philosophical breakthroughs can all occur in a frighteningly short space of time.

It's the very stuff of drama, inside the drama. The stakes are even higher when the people involved have invested themselves, personally and financially, in the show. Then, desperation is added to the mix. The agony increases as does the laughter.

I wanted to write something about what I'd observed of this over fifteen years as an actor. Taking Mr. Garrick's clue, I attempted to make my departure point a serious one. At the heart of the film I wanted to touch on the personal lives of the characters involved. The actors' melancholy, loneliness and isolation. Their ongoing relationship with failure, rejection and humiliation. Familiar feelings to many people but often concentrated in the lives of actors. Around this desire to observe human nature in absurd crisis, I tried to build the comedy. For my prime aim was to make people laugh.

The theatre as a metaphor for life's madness is hardly new. And movies that use the stories of particular productions to provide a microcosmic view of human nature abound. The "backstage" drama is almost a genre. I grew up watching them on television—Mickey Rooney and Judy Garland in *Babes in Arms*—"Why: we could do the show right here," they proclaimed, and then promptly gave us a dozen complicated dance numbers featuring thousands of people (all in the school gymnasium), which they couldn't possibly have had time to rehearse. I marvelled at it. There was Warner Baxter yelling at Ruby Keeler in *42nd Street* and Jack Benny farcing his way through a Nazi-infested Hamlet in *To Be or Not to Be*.

They had the magic of black-and-white photography. The sense of a heightened reality which seems to fit when describing the world of the theatre. But these movies talked of Broadway and other exotic locations. The shows involved were musicals.

My most regular theatrical experiences, by comparison, have been low-budget Shakespeares in places like Norwich (in a tent, incidentally). But that was partly the point, I suppose. This could be the farty British version, with its roots much more firmly in the soil of the Ealing Comedy tradition. The aspirations of the characters seem to remain the same regardless of the locale.

I wanted, in any case, to use something as famous and dangerously cliche-ridden as Hamlet, for the show within the show. It's a play that has obsessed me for the last twenty years, and one that most people have been exposed to in some form or other. Either in some misty cultural memory of a man in black tights with a skull or through TV advertisements for small cigars that bear the same name. It represents, for some, Shakespeare's greatest achievement, and for others its meaning is as remote as an ancient civilization. One of the characters asks how a fourteen-year-old in 1995 can connect or identify in any way with a four-hundred-year-old play about a depressed aristocrat. I've spent most of my career trying to answer the same question.

So is this screenplay pure autobiography? Well, I don't think so. It's certainly very personal. There is much of me in Joe (although not the terrible experience of a year's unemployment), but as the screenplay developed it started to belong to the actors involved.

I wrote it with many of them in mind, and once they were officially cast their contribution was enormous. It was the cumulative experience of this group that informed and changed the script. All the mad audition sequences come from life, as do many of the characters. The film itself was made in the spirit of the story. Everyone—actors and crew—received the same initial payment, and everyone who worked throughout the shoot received a profit participation. The very fact of this affected the tone of the final movie. The spirit of generous collaboration (not without the odd fit of temper) made for a shoot (of just twenty-one days) which, as Hamlet would say, held "the mirror up to nature."

The gap between life and art in this case was quite narrow. At times it made for an atmosphere of utter silliness, which anyone who passionately believes in the power of the theatre is also equally familiar with.

The ending takes us into different territory. Some will find it sentimental. It is. Actors are sentimental. It's one of our weaknesses. But I believe at times one of the gloriously silly ones. It may not translate into action on all occasions. Or overcome the vanity, greed and insecurity to which we are regularly and comically prey, but in this instance I wanted the happy ending, which we beggarly actors so long for, and rarely find.

I hope that elsewhere there is enough of the bitter irony that constitutes much of the actor's life to earn us our fictional place in the winter sun. For if this is a true valentine to the theatre and actors, it should be shot through with the (albeit unheroic) pain of the process. This was our serious intent in the business of this comedy, aimed above all at giving pleasure.

My everlasting thanks to the talented and kind group of collaborators who allowed me to have a go.

Kenneth Branagh

ABOUT THE AUTHOR

In 1988, Kenneth Branagh took the international film community by surprise with his direction, adaptation, and starring role in *Henry V*. The critically acclaimed film, his directing debut, won numerous nominations and awards including: Best Actor and Best Director Academy Award nominations; an Academy Award for Best Costume Design; a Best New Director award from the National Board of Review; a Best New Director award from the New York Critics Circle; two Felix Awards for Best Actor and Young European Film of the Year; a BAFTA Award for Best Director; and the Evening Standard Award for Best Film of 1989.

A Midwinter's Tale is Branagh's sixth feature film as a director. When it premiered under the title *In the Bleak Midwinter* at the 1995 Venice International Film Festival, it was awarded the Osella d'Oro. It then screened at the 1995 Boston Film Festival, where Branagh was awarded the Filmmaker Excellence Award. Branagh is currently starring in and directing his film version of *Hamlet*.

In a relatively brief career, Branagh has established himself as one of the most versatile artists of the day and is especially known as an interpreter of classic literature for the screen. His films are *Dead Again* (1991); *Peter's Friends* (1992), which won the Evening Standard Peter Sellers Award for Comedy; *Swan Song* (1992), an Academy Award-nominated short film; *Much Ado About Nothing* (1993), which was screened in competition at the Cannes Film Festival; *Mary Shelley's Frankenstein* (1994); and *A Midwinter's Tale* (1995).

Born in Belfast, Ireland, and raised in England, Branagh made his professional and West End debut in Julian Mitchell's *Another Country*, for which he won the Society of West End Theater's Award and the Plays and Players Award, both for the Most Promising Newcomer of 1982. His career has included such classic roles as Iago in Oliver Parker's film version of *Othello*; Hamlet, in a record-breaking run at the Royal Shakespeare Company; Coriolanus, at the Chichester Festival Theatre, which was coproduced by Chichester and his own Renaissance Theatre Company. He has also starred in other Shakespeare productions, among them: *Romeo and Juliet*, *Much Ado About Nothing*, *As You Like It*, and *Love's Labor's Lost*. As a director he has brought *Twelfth Night*, *Uncle Vanya*, and *The Life of Napoleon* to the stage, among others. Branagh has also taken leading roles in many British television productions, notably in *Strange Interlude*, *The Lady's Not for Burning,* and the series *Fortunes of War*.

Branagh's writing credits include adapting *Henry V* and *Much Ado About Nothing* for the screen and writing two plays: *Tell Me Honestly* and *Public Enemy*, produced for the Renaissance Theatre Company's first season.

A MIDWINTER'S TALE

by

KENNETH BRANAGH

Kenneth Branagh's *A Midwinter's Tale*
was produced and released in the United Kingdom
and outside of the United States under the title
In the Bleak Midwinter.

SHEPPERTON STUDIOS,
STUDIOS ROAD,
SHEPPERTON,
MIDDLESEX

Black.

The credits dissolve slowly on and off as we hear the
unmistakable voice of Noël Coward.

> The world for some years
> Has been sodden with tears
> On behalf of the acting profession.
>
> Each star
> Playing a part
> Seems to expect
> A purple heart.
>
> It's unorthodox
> To be born in a box
> But it needn't become an obsession.
>
> Let's hope we have no more to plague us
> Than three shows a night in Las Vegas.
>
> When I think of physicians
> And mathematicians
> Who don't earn a quart of the dough
> When I think of the miners
> And waiters in diners
> There's one thing I'm burning to know ...

But before we can launch into the jaunty chorus,

                                                      CUT.

1 INT. - DAY.   1

Mid-shot on JOE who speaks directly to camera. He is of
medium height, dark, wiry.

                    JOE
> It was late November, er ... I think
> ... and I was thinking about the whole
> Christmas thing, the birth of Christ,
> Wizard of Oz, family murders, and quite
> frankly I was depressed. I mean I'd always
> wanted to live my life like in a old movie
> - a sort of fairytale you know? Mind you,
> I suppose if you think that a lot of
> fairytales turn out to be nightmares, and
>   (MORE)

(CONTINUED)

1   CONTINUED: 1

JOE (Cont'd)

that a lot of old movies are crap, then
that's what I did. Er, the thing was, you
know the way doctors say that nervous
breakdowns can happen, very fast and dramatically; sort of big bang, or, there are
the other kind that happen very slowly,
over a period of time. Well I was thirty-
three years old, and er, this one started
when I was about seven months, and it had
just begun to get a grip ...

                                                    CUT.

Mr Coward's jaunty chorus finally begins as the remaining
CREDITS roll swiftly, white on black. The last credit dis-
appears and a legend proclaims:

PROLOGUE

'I HAVE TO TALK TO MY AGENT'

2   INT. RESTAURANT - DAY.   2

Mid-heated conversation between JOE and his agent MARGARET-
TA D'ARVILLE, laconic, smart dressing: part agent, part
therapist.

MARGARETTA

Darling. You're depressed that's all,
everyone gets depressed. For most people,
there's no happy, there's no sad, there's
just various stages of depressed. That's
life.

JOE

Well, not for me. Not anymore. Look,
please help me with this idea.

MARGARETTA

Darling, you tried it before. It was a
disaster.

JOE

Margy, I've been an actor now for eleven
years. If everything had gone according to
Laurence Olivier's book I would have known
triumph, disappointment and married a
beautiful woman. Instead I've known ted-
ium, humiliation and got shacked up with
the psycho from hell. Life has to change.

                                              (CONTINUED)

2   CONTINUED: 2

> **MARGARETTA**
>
> But not by committing professional sui-
> cide.
>
> **JOE**
>
> I have to do this play. I've given my life
> a deadline.
>
> **MARGARETTA**
>
> Look Christmas, wait till the New Year,
> give it some thought.
>
> **JOE**
>
> I have given it thought, 365 days' worth.

CUT.

3   EXT. STREET - DAY.   3

A busy London thoroughfare. MARGARETTA and JOE are walking
towards us. Talking across each other.

> **MARGARETTA**
>
> Alright, you get the £600 and my office
> and a phone for one week. Now, I want to
> be in on the casting and I can put an ad
> in *Theatre Weekly*, but better be careful
> we don't want law suits. But I'm warning
> you, at this time of year, everyone is
> doing Christmas shows or TV specials so
> all you are going to get is eccentrics,
> misfits and nutters.
>
> **JOE**
>
> Margy, I love you.

JOE kisses MARGARETTA.

> **MARGARETTA**
>
> Oh shush you silly little suicidal megalo-
> maniac you.
>
> **JOE**
>
> Margy, Margy, what about that film?
>
> **MARGARETTA**
>
> What film?
>
> **JOE**
>
> That stupid science-fiction film.
>
> **MARGARETTA**
>
> Ah yes, you said you weren't interested in
> that!

3   CONTINUED: 3

                              JOE
          I'm just curious.

                           MARGARETTA
          Well ... it was down to you and Dylan
          Judd.

     Pause.

                              JOE
          Dylan J ... I don't believe it ... I don't
          ... I'm ... I'm, I'm speechless ... I'm
                           MARGARETTA
                    (putting on her sunglasses)
          I'm so glad, I'm so glad you've regained
          your artistic soul darling, I really am.
          You mustn't let these little things bother
          you.

     She goes. He remains spluttering.

                              JOE
          Dylan Judd ... Dylan Judd ... he's ...
          he's short ...

                                                            CUT.

4   EXT. NEWSAGENTS - DAY.   4

     JOE dashes out of the shop, clutching his copy of *Theatre
     Weekly*.

     MARGARETTA is waiting in her Land Rover to review the ad.
     JOE clambers into the passenger seat.

                              JOE
                    (pointing out the ad)
          There, there.
                           MARGARETTA
                    (reading)
          AUDITIONS ... nice and big that's good.
          LIMITED ENGAGEMENT, dec 11th - dec 31st,
          HAMLET ... that's clear, simple, so far so
          good ... A CO-OPERATIVE EXPERIENCE
          ... do you have to use these phrases
          darling, it's not 1969 ...

                                                          (CONTINUED)

4   CONTINUED: 4

                         JOE
          ... People need to know it's an
          ensemble ...
                         MARGARETTA
          ... and that you're the biggest
          ensembler ...
                         JOE
          ... get on with it ... Please, please.
                         MARGARETTA
               (appalled)
          ... PROFIT-SHARE, 'SPIRIT SHARE' ... unbe-
          lievable.
                         JOE
          ... it's not about money ...
                         MARGARETTA
          ... or grammar ... ACCOMMODATION AND
          'INSPIRATION' ... can't you just say their
          digs are included ...
                         JOE
          ... They need to recognize the
          commitment ...
                         MARGARETTA
          ... what's this ... oh God ... 'six fellow
          journeymen to enter the gloomy dane' ...
                         JOE
          Oh no ... That's a mistake ... NO, NO IT
          SHOULD BE TO 'TO ENTER THE WORLD OF THE
          GLOOMY DANE ... '
                         MARGARETTA
          ... It hardly matters darling ... it fin-
          ishes with ... APPLY TO THE DIRECTOR AND
          SWEAT PRINCE ...
                         JOE
          ... Sweet, sweet, sweet prince ...
                         MARGARETTA
          Great darling. Expect a lot of new-age
          gays looking for a workout.

                                                          CUT.

Caption white on black:

                         ACT I
          'WHY ... WE COULD DO THE SHOW RIGHT HERE'

5   INT. AGENT'S OFFICE - DAY.   5

CLOSE-UP on JOE, sitting behind a desk. Music plays through
the following audition montage, which begins with JOE,
unused to this position of power, nervous and eager.
Desperate to make his fellows comfortable. His wide-eyed
and optimistic expression changes markedly as the succes-
sion of candidates passes before him through the tiny,
anonymous office.

MARGARETTA sits in the office throughout.

                    JOE

          It's terrific that you could come in
          ... thanks very much indeed. Now this is a
          really collaborative piece but ... if
          you'd ... like to do something, it doesn't
          have to be Shakespeare ... you know
          ... whatever ... this production wants to
          be extremely innovative in the way we
          communicate ...

We cut to a lycra-ed woman tap dancer who smiles a cheesy,
face-splitting grin on the other side of the desk. A string
around her neck holding flip-over cards which she turns as
she taps. Flip. The card reads 'THIS IS TO BE OR NOT TO
BE'. She taps,

                    JOE
              (genuinely amazed)
          Ah ... Ah ... Ah ... Ah ...
                  TAP DANCER
              (delighted)
          Thanks, I thought it would probably work.

MARGARETTA in shock.

                                              CUT.

CLOSE-UP on the contorted face of a young actor in hunchback mode giving the full dalek-ian version of Olivier's
Richard III.

                  YOUNG ACTOR
          'Now is the winter of our discontent
          Made glorious summer by this son of York.'

                                          (CONTINUED)

5 CONTINUED: 5

                              JOE
                    (rushing to the actor, all concern)
              I don't feel you've made it quite your
              own, you know ... Listen, let's just drop
              the voice, silly idea I know, and drop the
              hunch and the gestures OK?
                          YOUNG ACTOR
                    (eager)
              OK. Fine.

JOE goes back to his desk.

                              JOE
              Then let's just see what happens. Whenever
              you want, in your own time.

After great loosening-up preparations. He does it exactly
the same way.

                          YOUNG ACTOR
              'Now is the winter of our discontent
              Made glorious summer by this son of York.'

JOE ushers him out.

                              JOE
              Absolute transformation.
                          YOUNG ACTOR
              Oh, it felt great ...
                              JOE
              Thank you, thank you so much.
                          YOUNG ACTOR
              It was like something really freed up.
                              JOE
              You did, you freed right up.

                                                            CUT.

CLOSE-UP on HENRY WAKEFIELD, been there, seen that, done it
all, liked none of it type, loves the theatre and acting in
spite of himself. The child of an older school, he's a
decrepit cross between Henry Irving and Tony Hancock. He
drags heavily on a roll-up.

                       HENRY WAKEFIELD
              Henry Wakefield's the name love, known as
              Harry to those who wish to annoy me.

                                              (CONTINUED)

5   CONTINUED: (2)   5

                              JOE

          Whatever you prefer to be ...

                              HENRY

          Look love, I won't mess about. I hate
          these profit-share things. I want to play
          the King, right. I should have played it
          years ago but you's pays your money and
          puts up with your miserable bloody
          choices.

                              JOE

          Yes. Well it's a wonderful role -

                              HENRY

          Less of the director bullshit love - just
          say yes. Let's face it you're lucky to
          have me. From your ad this production's
          already about as promising as playing
          Rookery Nook on the Titanic, so don't
          waste my time sonny eh?

          See you at the read-through.

                                                           CUT.

CLOSE-UP on HENRY WAKEFIELD's ancient, glamourised oddly
angled Spotlight photo, being pinned to a wall with his
assigned character names below it - Claudius, Ghost,
Player-King.

                                                           CUT.

to Ultra Variety type Ventriloquist and dummy, hard to tell
them apart. Both sound like a strangulated Tommy Cooper.

                              DUMMY

          ... alas, poor Yorick, I knew him well.

                                                           CUT.

To MARGARETTA miming 'no' and 'he's mad'.

                              DUMMY

                         (insane)

          He likes us, he likes us, he thinks we're
          funny ...

                                                           CUT.

The face of an intense young actor, TOM NEWMAN. Vegetarian,
Planet-saving, Whale-rescuing, Trade-papers reading and,
finally and conclusively, self-absorbed. He is in earnest
flow, despite being intellectually challenged.

                                                    (CONTINUED)

5   CONTINUED: (3)

                    TOM
        ... but no, no, no, no, Hamlet isn't just
        Hamlet, oh no, no, oh no, Hamlet is me
        ... Hamlet is ... Bosnia, Hamlet is ...
        this desk ... Hamlet is the air, Hamlet is
        ... my grandmother, Hamlet is everything
        you've ever thought about sex, ... about
        ... about ... geology ...

                    JOE
    Geology?

                    TOM
                (flanneling)
    In a very loose sense of course.

                    JOE
    Can you fence?

                    TOM
    I adore to fence ... I live to fence ...
    in a sense I fence to live ...

                                        CUT.

Tom's picture goes up on the board. Underneath, Laertes,
Fortinbras, Messengers.

                                        CUT.

MAD WOMAN with two small hand puppets made from paper cups
being the Macbeths. She makes weird fanfare noises.

MARGARETTA making cut signs to JOE.

                    MAD WOMAN
    Have I got it?

                    JOE
    Well, ... we are going to see a lot of
    people ... extraordinary amount of people.
    I can't say until the end of the cycle ...

                                        CUT.

CLOSE UP of a page of SPOTLIGHT on the desk. Four pho-
tographs (all terrible) of the same actor in astonishingly
varied disguises. Despite oddly placed facial hair and
pipes, he gives the same expression in all four pho-
tographs. A look that says 'Hello, I'm barking mad but
harmless'. We tilt up to meet, live, the cosy features of
CARNFORTH GREVILLE, who strangely is giving Joe a look
which says 'Hello, I'm barking mad, but harmless'. Older

                                        (CONTINUED)

5 CONTINUED: (4)   5

than his years, with an affable calm that comes only to the
terminally eccentric.

                    CARNFORTH
        ... amazing isn't it ... little spirit
        gum and a little imagination ... one
        becomes totally unrecognisable.

JOE in shock.

                    CARNFORTH
        ... In my early days in rep they used to
        call me Carnforth 'Varied' Greville
        ... you know ... because of all the
        ... you know ...

                    JOE.
        Variety?

                    CARNFORTH
        Yes ... that's it, variety of characters.
        Yes.

                                          CUT.

CARNFORTH GREVILLE's photograph - Rosencrantz,
Guildenstern, Horatio and Bernardo.

                                          CUT.

TERRY DU BOIS, a man for whom the word camp was invented.

                    TERRY
        Well, Dorothy Drab's certainly made an
        impact in here dahling. I suppose it could
        be more dreary if you smeared the walls
        with sheep's shit, but it's hardly worth
        it. No, you keep it anonymous and suicidal
        darling.

A gobsmacked look from JOE who tries to get a word in.

        I'm not playing Polonius darling. Dirty
        Gerty's got my name on it. I'm here to
        play the Queen.

                    JOE
        Now look ...

                                          (CONTINUED)

5   CONTINUED: (5)   5

                          TERRY

        You haven't had a matronly cleavage near
        you all week. You're stuck for mummy and
        you are looking at the answer to your
        prayers. I'm clean, I'm conscientious and
        I travel with me own tits.

                          JOE

                    (hesitant)

        To be perfectly honest with you, I am a
        bit stuck and I do want the production to
        be free and experimental.

                          TERRY

        That's the way I feel about most things
        darling.

                                                    CUT.

TERRY's photograph takes its place - Gertrude.

                                                    CUT.

CLOSE UP on nervous, sweaty person. The man, at the top of
his voice, begins

                          BALDING MAN

        Muuule Traaaaaain!!!!

And as he launches into the verse, he beats, to the rhythm
of the song, an aluminium tray on his head, very hard.

                          BALDING MAN

        ... Clippity Cloppin, Clippity Cloppin,
        down the mountain trail ...

The face of a fervent young Scotsman.

                                                    CUT.

                          JOE.

        For me regional accents are not, no prob-
        lem at all ... they are vitally important
        in fact. There is no 'set' voice for
        Shakespeare ... that's ridiculous ...

The GLASWEGIAN begins to impersonate Olivier's hunchback.

                                              (CONTINUED)

5   CONTINUED: (6)   5

                         GLASWEGIAN
            I tried this, this morning.
            'Noi iz thah wuntre ov r diskantant
            Maid glorious summer bai that sun ov
            York'.

It is unintelligible. JOE tries to smile.

                                                          CUT.

To reveal VERNON SPATCH. Blonde, lithe, physique rubbery,
personality tough. Cheerful but uncompromising.

                         VERNON
            ... That's the advantage of being a child
            actor you see. I've already been in the
            business for seven centuries.
                         JOE
            It's certainly an impressive C.V.
                         VERNON
            Well, I'm not doing it anymore right? I've
            got to play someone older. Fourteen years
            on tour in Peter Pan can give you a com-
            plex.

                                                          CUT.

VERNON's picture - Polonius, Marcellus, 1st Gravedigger and
Osric.

                                                          CUT.

Standing opposite the desk is NINA RAYMOND, dark, strange.
She stares at JOE.

                         JOE
            Are your eyes quite alright?
                         NINA
            Perfect.
                         JOE
            It's just that you're not actually looking
            at me. You're looking just off to one
            side.
                         NINA
            Exactly.
                         JOE
            Oh?

                                                      (CONTINUED)

5 CONTINUED: (7)   5

                         NINA
          I often do that when I first meet people.
          I look off to the side ... to ... to watch
          their aura.

                         JOE.
     Their aura?

                         NINA.
          Their aura ... or as often as not just the
          bit of space next to them which can be
          very interesting. Can't it?

MARGARETTA give JOE a look, 'What?'
                         JOE
     Do you wear contact lenses?

                         NINA
     No, ... they're uncomfortable.

                         JOE
     Well, why don't you wear glasses?

                         NINA
                  (aggressive)
     I don't need them. (Beat.) Can I do my
     piece now? They said it didn't have to be
     Shakespeare.

                         JOE
     No.

                         NINA
     Oh good, this is Debbie Harry then.

She begins to sing. Very serious. Tone-deaf and with a rou-
tine that is highly original.

                         NINA
     'Once I found love and it was a gas, soon
     found out had a heart of glass. Seemed
     like the real thing, only to find what you
     mistrust, love's gone blind.'

With this she kicks one leg in the air, hits the underside
of the desk and ends up ass over elbow.

                                                     CUT.

JOE is pinning NINA's photo to the wall of shame - Ophelia,
Fortinbras Captain, 2nd Gravedigger, Voltimand, Cornelius.

                                                     CUT.

6   INT. AGENT'S OFFICE - END OF DAY.   6

      JOE at the casting board with MARGARETTA.

> JOE
>
> It was always going to be difficult at
> this time of the year and at such short
> notice, but we've got a group of people
> who are really hungry to do it.

> MARGARETTA
>
> They're hungry because they haven't worked
> this century.

> JOE
>
> Neither have I.

Beat.

> MARGARETTA
>
> Touché. How am I going to get people in
> the business down to this God-forsaken
> venue?

> JOE
>
> It's not for those kind of people.

> MARGARETTA
>
> What, you mean employer kind of people?

Beat.

> JOE
>
> Look, it's a one-off production by a group
> of (I suspect) mad, but passionate people
> who are really hungry to do it, who will
> be performing it in a place that really
> needs us. If we do it well and honestly
> everything else will follow.

> MARGARETTA
>
> Ooo I love it when you go all visionary.
> (Pause.) Oh, you know you really were
> close to that movie.

> JOE
>
> Oh really?

> MARGARETTA
>
> Really. And now Dylan Judd's agent has
> gone all grand and is asking for millions.
> Such a mistake.

Beat.

(CONTINUED)

6   CONTINUED: 6

                              JOE

            You'll come won't you?

                          MARGARETTA

            We'll see. I have a feeling it might be
            worth travelling a very long way for Terry
            Du Bois's Gertrude.

                                                          CUT.

7   EXT. PHONEBOX - DAY.   7

     MOLLY, JOE's sister, in a country phone box. We cut back-
     wards and forwards between her and JOE, in the office.

                             MOLLY

            So when exactly are you going to get to
            the church?

8   INT. AGENT'S OFFICE - DAY.   8
                              JOE

            Sunday lunchtime, I hope. Depends on the
            transport captain.

9   INT. PHONEBOX - DAY.   9
                             MOLLY

            Why? Who's that?

10   INT. AGENT'S OFFICE - DAY.   10
                              JOE

            Me.

11   INT. PHONEBOX - DAY.   11
                             MOLLY

            You're not really going to drive that old
            heap are you? With live people in it?

12   INT. AGENT'S OFFICE - DAY.   12
                              JOE

            Well with actors in it, there is a differ-
            ence. Anyway I've no choice. If I'm not
            paying them any money I've got to look
            after them. Look, I'll see you at the top
            of the hill.

13   INT. PHONEBOX - DAY.   13

MOLLY

Joe, Joe, What do you mean, top of the
hill?

14   INT. AGENT'S OFFICE - DAY.   14

JOE

By the church gates. Listen, listen, I
have to go, I've got get the food for
Sunday. I'm catering manager too. See you
love, bye.

15   INT. PHONEBOX - DAY.   15

MOLLY

No, no Joe, hang on. You don't mean.
(Putting down the receiver.)

Oh God.
(Exiting the phonebox.)

Oh Christ.

16   EXT. EMPTY CAR PARK - DAY.   16

Sunday Morning. JOE's 'characterful' Volkswagen Passat
Estate, packed with his new troupe.

Camera outside the car, looking from the bonnet through the
windscreen to the packed car. JOE in the driver's seat.
HENRY in the passenger's. TERRY in the middle of the second
row with CARNFORTH and NINA either side. TOM and VERNON
squeezed like chickens into the estate bit.

NINA V/O

Shall I navigate?

ALL V/O

NO!

JOE V/O

So everybody alright back there?

Then in unison with camp actor complicity they drawl with
languid emphasis.

ALL V/O

Mahvellous, Daahling.

(CONTINUED)

16   CONTINUED: 16

They backfire into the sunset as we

                                                      CUT.

17   EXT. COUNTRY LANE - DAY.   17

We hear the in-transit dialogue as the car drives by a sign
proclaiming their final destination, the village of Hope.

                    TOM V/O
          Oh look, what a beautiful name.
                    NINA V/O
          I think it's a sign.
                    HENRY V/O
          Yes, love, it's a road sign.
                    TOM V/O
          I think it's symbolical.

                                                      CUT.

18   EXT. COUNTRY CAR PARK - DAY.   18

They get out of the car.

                    JOE
          Now look we can't actually get the vehicle
          any closer than this. So we'll have to
          carry the stuff from here. We'll get the
          rest later. It is a lovely short walk.
                    TOM
          And up a hill too, how wonderful, perfect
          after the journey like that.

They start to walk up the hill. If HENRY's looks could
kill.

                    HENRY WAKEFIELD
          Wonderful!

                                                      CUT.

19   EXT. HILL PATH - DAY.   19

The party make their way up the hill, TOM striding ahead of
them, JOE helping NINA, who is walking up the hill on her

                                              (CONTINUED)

19   CONTINUED:

roller blades. VERNON shooting his video, HENRY roll-up-
ing, TERRY mincing, CARNFORTH musing. Various degrees of
struggle with bags.

> JOE
>
> We were brought up around here. It was
> such a beautiful church. Even us kids
> liked going.

> NINA
>
> It's such a shame it's fallen into disuse.

> VERNON
>
> Like most of this company.

> TERRY
>
> Speak for yourself, you cheeky witch.

> HENRY
>
> I must say it's wonderfully accessible for
> our audience.

> CARNFORTH
>
> Ah. 'The road is long, though firm and
> strong, and tinkly, like a dinner gong.'

> HENRY WAKEFIELD
>
> Did you just make that up?

> CARNFORTH
>
> No, I think it's by ... erm ... no
> ... actually ... I think I did just
> make it up.

CUT.

20   EXT. PICTURESQUE CHURCH - DAY.   20

They gaze on admiringly.

> VERNON
>
> Actually, that is terrific isn't it? Like
> out of Wuthering Heights or something.

> NINA
>
> It's so romantic, and yet so sad.

> TERRY
>
> Yes, it's got a sort of feminine sadness,
> hasn't it Nina? I could make my first
> entrance from outside.

> CARNFORTH
>
> It's certainly worth the trudge isn't it?

(CONTINUED)

20   CONTINUED:

                              TOM

          And a fantastic position up here on the
          hill. There must be some tremendous runs
          to be had around here.

                    HENRY WAKEFIELD

          It's certainly very atmospheric being sur-
          rounded by dead people.

                         VERNON

          Not much of a change from your normal
          audiences then Harry.

                         HENRY

          Henry.

                          JOE

                    (evangelic)

          Well, this is it folks, the old hill
          church of Hope. We're not just doing a
          play. We're here on a mission. To save
          this place. To get the developer out and
          the people back in.

                       MOLLY V/O

          Joe! Joe!

                          JOE

          Ah, this is my sister, Molly.

MOLLY approaching breathless from up the hill. She runs
into JOE's arms - he lifts her up in a hug.

                          JOE

          How are you?

Putting MOLLY back down.

                         MOLLY

          Oh God, you! I thought you'd got it wrong.
          It's not this church. Everybody loves this
          church. It's the big one on the edge of
          the village.

They turn as one to face the horrible truth. Beat.

                          JOE

          Not the big horrible red one?

                         MOLLY

          Yes.

                                             CUT.

21   EXT. UGLY RED CHURCH - DAY.   21

Wide shot. The car now parked outside the big ugly church.
The group starts to unpack the luggage again.

                    HENRY WAKEFIELD
        Well, that really is a dog of a church.

                    VERNON
        Graphically, actually it isn't bad, all
        those nice verticals.

                    TOM
        It's so much flatter round here. Not
        nearly so good for working the heart rate.

                    TERRY
        Well at least, we can go to town on my
        dressing room in here love, I do need
        space for my talent.

                    VERNON
        Space to find it.

                    TERRY
        Shut up.

                    HENRY
        Look, haven't we seen enough? We'll be
        sick of the sight of the place. Can't we
        just go to the digs?

                    JOE
        These are the digs. It's the only way we
        can afford to do it.

                    MOLLY
        We've got loads of stuff - food, heaters,
        sleeping bags, futons.

                    CARNFORTH
        Actually, I'm not terribly keen on
        Japanese food.

                                                    CUT.

22   INT. CHURCH - DAY.   22

Wide shot as the group enters and slowly explores.

                    NINA
        Gosh, it's incredibly atmospheric.

                    VERNON
        And damp.

                                              (CONTINUED)

22 CONTINUED:

> JOE
>
> I remember this place. We used to get
> dragged in here once a month on a Sunday
> night for 'extra' religion.

> MOLLY
>
> Oh yes, Mum and Dad made sure we got our
> money's worth alright.

> CARNFORTH
>
> And have you kept it up?

> TERRY
>
> Carnforth, watch your language.

> TOM
>
> He means the faith, have you kept up the
> faith.

They walk down the nave together.

> No, it's terribly hard. I mean, I'm
> tremendously spiritual, but it's still
> very difficult for me to meditate for more
> than an hour each day.

> HENRY WAKEFIELD
>
> Yes, I expect that's about all Buddha can
> take from you isn't it?

> NINA
>
> So Molly, why doesn't anyone use this
> place anymore?

> MOLLY
>
> Well they do, or rather they did until
> this bloody developer got hold of it. I
> mean basically a lot of people have aban-
> doned Hope.

> HENRY
>
> I know how they feel love.

In walks, very slowly, FADGE. She is clearly communing with
something other worldly. Cloths in hair and an ensemble of
bizarre bits, she reduces the others to awed silence. She
moves as if re-enacting Grasshopper's walk across the rice
paper in Kung Fu.

> TOM
>
> Ooo what drama! Is this the landlord?

> JOE
>
> Oh, right, right. Let me introduce you.
> Our designer. This is Fadge.

(CONTINUED)

22   CONTINUED: (2)

                    NINA

Did he say Vadge?

                    TOM

I'm glad she uses the abbreviation.

                    FADGE

          (she stops)

FADGE darling, Fuh, Fuh, Fuh, give it an
F.

                    TERRY

I think it's a bit early in the day for
that darling.

                    TOM

Is this entire production going to be con-
ducted through a stream of innuendo?

                    NINA

Is there a surname Fadge?

                    VERNON

Yes, is it Fadge Smith? or Fadge
Fadginton?
or ...

                    FADGE

Just Fadge darling. (she stops) You know
this place is incredible. I feel something
very powerful here. Very strange and powerful.

                    NINA

Powerful and strange, I feel that too
Fadge.

                    VERNON

Powerful and strange and damp.

                    JOE

I was just saying Fadge, there's some marvellous opportunities here for -

                    FADGE

You see, we must make the design all about
Space. People in space, things in space,
women in space, men in space.

                    TOM

So we'd be sort of spacemen?

                    FADGE

In a sense.

                                        CUT.

23   INT. CRYPT - DAY.   23

Campbeds, heaters, a rough dorm.

                         VERNON
          So Carnforth, we get to sleep in the
          crypt. Do you think they might be trying
          to imply something about our acting?

                         CARNFORTH
          What, that it's a bit cryptic?

                         VERNON
          No, that it's dead.

                         CARNFORTH
          I don't know, I've seen worse in the army.

                         VERNON
          Were you in the army?

                         CARNFORTH
                    (thinks)
          Um ... No, not strictly speaking, no, but
          plays about the army, certainly. (Then
          rather nervously.) Vernon, do you think
          the boss would be offended if I popped out
          to recce the local hostelry, in lieu of
          this evening meal?

                         VERNON
          I don't know Carnforth. Why don't you ask
          him?

He leaves.

                                                  CUT.

24   INT. KITCHEN - DAY.   24

TERRY and MOLLY unpacking food.

                         TERRY
          We're talking about actors, darling, not
          civilians. Discipline is what they need.

                         MOLLY
          But you're not here for long. Really,
          it'll sort itself out.

                                            (CONTINUED)

24   CONTINUED: 24

> TERRY
>
> Twenty-one days love, sixty-three meals
> and eight trillion cups of tea. I don't
> know how many ass-wipes that runs to, but
> you don't want to be the one holding the
> loo roll, you'll take my advice. We'll
> draw up the cleaning and cooking rota now.
>
> MOLLY
>
> It's so long since I've spent time with
> Joe. I'd forgotten how actors behave. This
> is just like being in the Boy Scouts.
>
> TERRY
>
> Don't say that love. My pants will never
> dry.

                                                        CUT.

25   INT. CHURCH - DAY.   25

Henry, agitated, striding through the chapel, JOE trying to
keep up with him.

> HENRY
>
> I don't see why I have to share with the
> pouffe, love.
>
> JOE
>
> Oh, come on now Harry.
>
> HENRY
>
> Henry.
>
> JOE
>
> We're people of the world. A person's sex-
> uality is irrelevant.
>
> HENRY
>
> I couldn't care less if he shags hamsters
> or not. They're all the same. The entire
> British Theatre's dominated by the class
> system and a bunch of Oxbridge Homos.
>
> JOE
>
> I don't think Terry's Oxbridge.
>
> HENRY
>
> Well, it hardly matters, they're all drama
> Queens. I hope your Gertrude's a quiet
> woman.

(CONTINUED)

> JOE
> (stricken)
>
> Yes, ... I wanted to have a word with you
> about that actually ...

> HENRY
>
> When does she arrive, by the way? I hope
> she's not going to be late for the read-
> through.

They walk up to what will clearly be the 'stage'.

> JOE
>
> We should probably find five minutes
> before then, just to explain my concept of
> your Queen.

> HENRY
>
> It's not bad though is it? The stage feels
> good, you can command the audience. Henry
> Irving would have loved this ...

The smell of Dr. Footlights has suddenly transported Henry.
His posture changes. He looks out, eyes alight into some
imaginary, darkened auditorium. He begins to speak, nor-
mally at first and then as he quotes, he moves into a barely intelligible rendition of Henry Irving.

> 'Eet eez the cahz, eet eez the cahz, may
> sool, let me naht name it to you, you
> chaysd stahz, eet eez the cahz'.

He breaks out of the spell.

> Irving as he would have played Othello,
> love. Very strange gestures, but totally
> hypnotic.

Beat.

> JOE
>
> Look are you going to be OK with the bed-
> room arrangements? We could ask somebody
> to move.

> HENRY
>
> Alright, alright, I'll stay there. I can
> always sleep with me ass in a bucket.

                                                    CUT.

26   INT. UPSTAIRS GALLERY (GIRLS' BEDROOM) - DAY.   26

NINA unpacking. FADGE sketching.

                    NINA
          Oh, Hamlet at Christmas! With a group of
          like-minded artists in a rough but
          thrillingly real location. I can't think
          of anything that would make this job bet-
          ter.

                    FADGE
          A salary?

NINA tries to look at FADGE's drawings and model.

                    NINA
          Is that the design for the ... ?

FADGE quickly hugs the design to her.

                    FADGE
          It's not finished yet.
                    NINA
          Sorry.

NINA goes to her bag.

                    NINA
          Where did I put my moisturizer?

Beat.

                    FADGE
          You can call me 'Fuh'.
                    NINA
          What?
                    FADGE
          It's a nickname. Really close friends call
          me 'Fuh'.
                    NINA
               (slowly)
          Oh, well I'm very touched that you should
          allow me to use it ... I mean it's
          slightly harder to say than Fadge but
          it's beautiful ... 'Fuh' ... thank you.

26 CONTINUED: 26

NINA has found her cream and starts to apply it liberally
to her face.

> FADGE
>
> Why are you rubbing low calorie mayonnaise
> into your face?

CUT.

27 INT. CHURCH - NIGHT.   27

Wide shot. Trestle table. Everyone gathered round. Chilli
consumed. Red wine being enjoyed.

> VERNON
>
> Here's to Molly, Cheers!

A chorus of 'Well done, Molly' etc.

> CARNFORTH
>
> That's rather an acceptable little
> Chianti.

> HENRY
>
> Well, you've certainly given it a good
> road test, haven't you? You carry on
> drinking like this, it'll affect next
> year's harvest.

> JOE
>
> Actually, it is just worth talking a lit-
> tle about the food and drink situation.

We start to track along the table.

> VERNON
>
> Yes, when do we get our expenses, love?

> JOE
>
> Well, the point is I suppose that the most
> economic way of doing this is to operate
> our household budget from a central fund.

> VERNON
>
> You mean there are no expenses?

> JOE
>
> Not in the conventional sense.

> VERNON
>
> Is there another sense?

(CONTINUED)

27 CONTINUED: 27

                    HENRY

Well there's the crooked-bastard-who-
didn't-tell-us-before-we-got-the-job sense.

                    NINA

Now that's not fair. You wanted this job.
This is Joe's own money. He must spend it
how he thinks fit.

                    TERRY

Here, here.

                    NINA

This was a very generous meal.

                    TOM

Yes, the chilli was very nice but it really has to be the last red meat I have. I
mean already I'm going to have to detox
and irrigate. Colonically this has set me
right back.

                    JOE

Yes, sorry Tom, we'll all bear that in
mind as we implement the cooking roster.
Now Molly, thank God is going to do the
shopping for supplies, but we probably
will need to be economic with our provi-
sions.

                    HENRY

I think she means you've drunk our entire
Christmas wine allowance Mr Greville.

                    CARNFORTH

I hope not.

                    TERRY

                 (to HENRY)

Oh, leave her alone, Mrs Grumpy. I think
Nancy Nerves is rattling your bars about
tomorrow isn't she?

                    NINA

Yes, I'm nervous too. My stomach's full of
snakes. You know, some people get butter-
flies in their tummy, I get sort of snake
things.

                    VERNON

Those are your intestines love.

The camera has come to stop with FADGE in the foreground in
a trance.

                                              (CONTINUED)

27 CONTINUED: (2)   27

                              FADGE
          I can feel my nipples stiffening.

All heads turn to look.

                              FADGE
          It's a good sign. A very good sign.

More silence.

          Hard and quick. Hard and quick. If it
          happens the night before a production - I
          feel it to be a tremendous omen.

More silence.

                              TERRY
          Well, we're never short of a shock from Mr
          Mad are we?

                              MOLLY
          Excuse me, what is all this? Calling boys
          by girls' names? I'm completely lost.

                              TERRY
          Camp, darling. Theatrical camp. Banter.
          Keeps us all on the straight and narrow.
          Put a girl's name in front of any word,
          just to spice up your sentences. And
          always refer to a man as a she and a woman
          as a he. For example if I were to comment
          on Harry over there.

                              HENRY
          Henry.

                              TERRY
          I might say, 'Oo Mandy Misery's shafted
          Mrs Wakefield good and proper hasn't she?'

                              MOLLY
          I see.

                              TERRY
          Well you will darling. You never know,
          there might be a little more campery
          before the first night.

They all react to that.

28   INT. KITCHEN - NIGHT.   28

    TOM, MOLLY, NINA, FADGE and JOE. Washing and clearing away.

> MOLLY
>
> The point is there is nowhere for people
> to go, apart from the pub. If they can
> afford it. I mean, there's no village
> hall, there's no arts centre. I mean, we
> need this place to give people a focus.
> Prove to the council that there is a
> community worth maintaining. That there
> is a community.

> NINA
>
> Oh, then it would be wonderful if it was a
> great production.

> TOM
>
> Don't feel under any pressure Joe.

> MOLLY
>
> What is the show anyway? That bugger
> wouldn't even tell me. I hope it's
> something Christmassy, a comedy.

Beat.

> TOM
>
> It's *Hamlet*.

Beat.

> MOLLY
>
> Great. Hello kids. Do stop watching Mighty
> Morphin Power Rangers and come and watch
> a four-hundred-year-old play about a
> depressed aristocrat. I mean it's some-
> thing you can really relate to.

> JOE
>
> We've got our work cut out.

> MOLLY
>
> Who's playing Hamlet?

Beat.

> Oh no. That's bloody typical of you. It's
> so bloody boring.

JOE picks MOLLY up and carries her out of the kitchen.

(CONTINUED)

28   CONTINUED: 28

                              JOE
          Come on Molly, I'll take you home. You can
          walk off your disappointment.

NINA runs off after them.

                              NINA
          Can I come too? Just for the air.

                                                              CUT.

29   EXT. PICTURESQUE HILLSIDE CHURCH - NIGHT.   29

NINA and JOE returning from MOLLY's. A romantic silhouette
of the building. JOE in remote reflective mood. NINA, a
good listener.

                              JOE
          I hope you didn't mind coming this route.
          It's on our way home.
                              NINA
          Not at all. It's a chance to calm down
          after all the excitement. I couldn't have
          got to sleep right away.
                              JOE
          I just wanted to see this place again, you
          know. I'd set my heart on it.
                              NINA
          The other church is much more practical.
                              JOE
          I know, but this is where I grew up. It's
          just typically stupid of me not to have
          checked properly with Moll. Charging away
          as usual.
                              NINA
          That's enthusiasm. It's important. Not
          many people have it like you.
                              JOE
          I hope I can keep it up.
                              NINA
          I beg your pardon!
                              JOE
          Don't you start.

Beat.

                                                        (CONTINUED)

29 CONTINUED: 29

                              NINA
          Are you scared about tomorrow?
                              JOE
          Absolutely petrified. Right now I wish I'd
          got that stupid part in that stupid film
          and just had to turn up for six months in
          a funny suit and drink tea all day.
                              NINA
          Look, we're all right behind you. You
          won't fail.
                              JOE
          I did once before, you know. Fadge and I
          both. Different shows. Same bull at a gate
          mentality. Complete cock-up. All money
          lost, all confidence lost with it. The day
          it went bust my fiancée left me for another
          man. Wonderful timing. Only an actress can
          carry that off. No offence. I shouldn't be
          talking to you like this, should I?
                              NINA
          I'm flattered that you can confide in me.
          Martin always says that if you can face
          your troubles and fears and just acknowl-
          edge them, then you're halfway to letting
          them fly away. I always try to remember
          that.
                              JOE
          That's good advice. Who's Martin?
                              NINA
          My husband.

                                                          CUT.

Caption, white on black:

                              ACT II
               'THERE'S NO BUSINESS LIKE SHOWBUSINESS!'

30 INT. CHURCH - DAY.   30

     Wide shot of the group gathered around a trestle table for
     the read-through. FADGE is sitting on the stage overlooking
     the cast and sketching.

                                                      (CONTINUED)

30 CONTINUED: 30

                          JOE

          Right! This is obviously a very exciting
          moment. We're about to embark on this
          voyage of discovery. I'd like to talk a
          little about Hamlet.

          Now I see it as a very dark play -

                          TOM

          I see it as a very long play, darling.
          Sally Scissors is going to appear we hope?

                          JOE

          Yes, yes. I've got a lot of cuts, but what
          I'd like to do for the benefit of this
          read-through is to read the whole thing.

                          HENRY

          Oh great, we've only got ten days to
          rehearse but let's spend fifteen hours
          reading the whole bloody thing on day one.

                          JOE

          I'll give you the cuts directly after-
          wards.

                          NINA

          It's vital that we read the whole thing
          once.

                      CARNFORTH AND TOM

          Here, here.

                          JOE
                     (hypertense)
          Right, right, rather than waste any more
          time, you know on speeches and things, I
          would like to say at this stage, please
          enjoy the reading. I mean, don't feel
          obliged to give, you know, performances. I
          don't want that, but do avoid mumbling and
          just throwing it away - let's really hear
          the play. Let's really listen to each
          other. And relax. OK. Off we go -

Various members of the cast start to light cigarettes.

                          TOM

          Can I just mention smoking. I think it
          would be a really good idea. If this was a
          non-smoking read-through.

The atmosphere could be cut with a knife.

30 CONTINUED: (2)   30

                              JOE

          Right, right, No, if we could all be sen-
          sitive to that. Thanks very much Tom. OK.
          OK.

                                                    CUT.

31 INT. CHURCH - DAY.   31

                          CARNFORTH

          'Who's there?'

                            TERRY

                      (as Gertrude)

          'Good Hamlet, cast thy nighted colour off,
          And let thine eye look like a friend on
          Denmark.'

    HENRY in shock. Yes, Gertrude will be played by a man.

                            TERRY

          'Do not for ever with thy vailed lids
          Seek for thy noble father in the dust'.

    HENRY fuming, starts to roll-up a cigarette.

    We CUT as Noël Coward treats us to another chorus of biting
    wit to accompany our

32 READ-THROUGH MONTAGE: 32

    Why must the show go on?
    The room is sure not immutable,
    It might be wiser
    And more suitable just to close
    If you are in the throes
    Of personal grief and private woes

    Why stifle a sob
    While doing your job
    When if you lose your head
    You go out and grab a comfortable cab
    and go right home to bed

    Because you're not giving us much fun
    This laugh-cry-laugh routine's been overdone
    Hats off to show-folks
    For smiling when they're blue
    But more cameo po-folks

                                                    (CONTINUED)

32 CONTINUED: 32

    Are sick of smiling through
    And if you're out cold,
    Too old and most of your teeth have gone.

    Why must the show go on?
    I sometimes wonder
    Why must the show go on?

    Montage close-ups of nervous hands, fiddling with sweet
    packets, lighters, matches and cigarettes. Tapping feet.
    Script pages turning. One by one the cast begins to smoke.
    TOM tries to avoid it. MOLLY hides a yawn. FADGE tweaks her
    nipples.

    We end on a close-up of the last page of the play, then to
    a wide-shot of the entire company engulfed in cigarette
    smoke. The cast leaves the table coughing.

33 EXT. CHURCHYARD - DAY.   33

    The side doors of the church open and out pour the company
    for a coffee break. They are led by an irate HENRY followed
    by a grovelling JOE.

                        HENRY
            I can't stand pouffes!
                        JOE
            Henry -
                        HENRY
            Gertrude was not written as a shirtlifter.
                        JOE
            Shakespeare himself was probably bisexual.
                        HENRY
            Bollocks!
                        JOE
            It's an Elizabethan concept, it'll free up
            a whole part of the show.
                        HENRY
            A dyke I could have coped with, I don't
            mind the odd diesel, but I'm not having me
            tongue down that.

    They stomp away out of shot, but the galloping duo continue to
    dance in and out of the back of the frame as the rest of the

                                                        (CONTINUED)

scene goes on. The rest of the cast perches for a coffee.

> TERRY
>
> Methinks the lady doth protest too much,
> dahling.

> VERNON
>
> He's old school, love. He's just trying to
> prove that he's really twenty-nine, with
> six testicles and a four-foot dick.

> CARNFORTH
>
> (tentatively)
>
> Look chaps, I'm just nipping down to the
> ... post office for a quick ... stamp.

> TOM
>
> I cannot believe the cuts, I cannot
> believe the cuts, I cannot believe the
> cuts.

> VERNON
>
> Can you believe the cuts Tom?

> TOM
>
> No, I can't believe them.

> NINA
>
> Tom, you're playing all those parts. I
> mean, that's the real challenge isn't it?
> To make them all exciting and different.

> VERNON
>
> And brief.

> TOM
>
> Exactly. I'm going to speak to my agent.

> TERRY
>
> That's right, darling, threaten to walk.
> The management will quake in their boots.

> NINA
>
> Oh please don't leave, Tom. I think you'd
> be a wonderful Laertes.

> TOM
>
> Well I have put quite a lot of work into
> it actually. Normally I'd have tried to
> spend a month in Denmark to get it right.

> VERNON
>
> So what did you do this time?

(CONTINUED)

                              TOM

Well, I borrowed this book on the Eiffel
Tower ... You know in the play he goes to
France? I just wanted an image in my head.

                              TERRY

Well there's plenty of room for it, darling.

The noise of HENRY and JOE arguing is still at fever pitch.

                              MOLLY

Is Joe alright?

                              TERRY

Oh, he's fine love, he's just humouring
Mrs Wakefield.

                              MOLLY

Will he leave? Is it always like this on
the first day of a play?

                              NINA

It's sort of political I think.

                              VERNON

Marking out territory.

                              TERRY

Yes, she's a ruthless step-daughter that
one.

                              MOLLY

Did you enjoy the read-through Fadge?

                              FADGE

I thought it was extraordinary. And also,
in a strange way banal.

                              VERNON

Does that mean you've decided on an extraordinary banal design.

                              FADGE

I can't - I never decide at this stage.
One has to remain open.

                              VERNON

Open and indecisive?

                              FADGE

No, - I -

                              NINA

Oh, stop teasing, Vernon. I can't wait to
see the set model ... Fuh.

                                              (CONTINUED)

33   CONTINUED: (3)   33

                    VERNON
              (to Terry)
     Fur?

                    TERRY
     Did she say Fur?

                                                           CUT.

34   INT. CHURCH - DAY.   34

    Close-up on the Set Model being revealed from under a box
    by FADGE. It is a cardboard replica of the church's inte-
    rior. The cast stare silently. NINA's face in very close to
    it. HENRY, placated, is nevertheless in a roll-up-sulk.
    Long pause.

                    CARNFORTH
     Um ... Isn't this ... um ... (He burps.)
     pardon.

                    TERRY
     You'll have to go easy licking those
     stamps at lunchtime Mrs Greville.

                    CARNFORTH
     Yes, but ... this is sort of exactly
     ... where we are ... isn't it?

                    FADGE
     Exactly.

                    TOM
     Brilliant.

                    VERNON
     So what's the design?

                    FADGE
     Smoke.

                    NINA
     Smoke?

                    FADGE
     People in space, in smoke.

                    HENRY.
     Oh Christ.

                    FADGE.
     This building does everything else. Smoke
     gives us atmosphere, mystery.

                    VERNON
     Bronchitis.

                                              (CONTINUED)

34 CONTINUED: 34

                         TERRY
          What about period then, darling?

                         FADGE
          Joe ... ?

                         JOE
          Well, I think we should create the period.
          I mean I don't think it should be
          Elizabethan, that would be ridiculous.

                         TOM
          Although, it is an Elizabethan play isn't
          it?

                         HENRY
          Oh, don't bring up the tedious details
          love.

                         JOE
          It should be no period, it should be our
          period. When everyone's come up with con-
          tributions for character and costume, the
          period and style will emerge. That's the
          nature of this collaboration.

                         VERNON
          Is 'cop-out' one word or two?

                         NINA
          I think you're being a naughty cynical
          sausage there, Vernon.

          Major camp 'shock' reaction from everyone.

                         JOE
          Yes, thank you Nina. We'll be having those
          discussions this afternoon about character
          and costume to set us all off on the right
          foot. We'll start rehearsals properly
          tomorrow with the first scene of the play.

                         TERRY
          Starting with the first scene? Oo she's so
          radical.

                         JOE
          Shut up bitch.

                                                  CUT.

35   EXT. FADGE'S VAN - AFTERNOON.   35

FADGE pulling out costumes, lights and props from the back
of her van. Talking to herself.

                    FADGE

          Bring everything with me. That's what Joe
          said. And the style with emerge.
          Hopefully.

                                              CUT.

36   INT. CHURCH - AFTERNOON.   36

A montage of the afternoon's work. The camera remains in
one position throughout. We jump cut. Manic activity in the
back of all these scenes. TERRY is with a nervous FADGE at
the costume rail.

                    TERRY

          I wear me own frocks love. I bring me
          own breasts. You look after the other
          children.

                                              CUT.

JOE and CARNFORTH talking.

                    CARNFORTH

          Yes, the thing is Joe, I noticed that I'm
          actually playing two characters that
          appear on stage at the same time, as it
          were ... ?

                                              CUT.

JOE and TOM.

                    TOM

          Actually Joe, I just wondered if I could
          mention the cuts. I think they are bril-
          liant, brilliant, so clever what you have
          done. It's just that Laertes has lost four
          key lines.

                                              CUT.

Back to JOE and CARNFORTH.

                    CARNFORTH

          Perhaps you maybe planned something, per-
          haps with mirrors?

                                              CUT.

                                         (CONTINUED)

36 CONTINUED: 36

Back to TOM and JOE.

                         TOM
          Just wondered if at some point you might
          consider reinstating them.
                         JOE
          Well, no,
                         TOM
          No, let me do it for you -
          'Oh Hamlet!'

                                                        CUT.

HENRY with his trousers off being measured by FADGE.

                         HENRY
          Are you going to be much longer? It's
          freezing in here.

                                                        CUT.

JOE and CARNFORTH.

                         JOE
          It's more a movement thing that I envis-
          aged.
                         CARNFORTH
          Movement? ... ah ...
                         JOE
          Fadge will help you.

                                                        CUT.

Back to JOE and TOM. The latter finishing his excerpt with
a flourish.

                         TOM
          Do you see what I mean?

                                                        CUT.

HENRY with trousers off, having his inside leg measured.

                         HENRY
          Careful, Careful.

                                                        CUT.

                                                  (CONTINUED)

36 CONTINUED: (2)   36

VERNON crosses frame with his video camera.

                                                        CUT.

HENRY crosses frames in the opposite direction.

                    HENRY
          Can't we get the frocks sorted out!

                                                        CUT.

JOE and TOM.

                    TOM
          And then I think he could rip his shirt
          off and abseil down from the organ for
          'where is my father'. They do some wonder-
          ful body oils now.

                                                        CUT.

NINA and FADGE race through shot.

                    NINA
          I don't want her to wear glasses.

                    FADGE
          You practically fell over the balcony get-
          ting into bed last night.

TOM rubbing oil into his bare chest.

                    TOM
          Doesn't the light read on this?

                                                        CUT.

JOE talking to VERNON.

                    VERNON
          I think a big nose would be great ... Did
          you see Cyrano de Bergerac ... ? That kind
          of size.

                                                        CUT.

                    HENRY
          I want huge shoulder pads. He's got to be
          butch.

                                                        CUT.

37   INT. JOE'S OFFICE - NIGHT.   37

JOE and MOLLY working at opposite ends of a trestle table
in front of the altar - JOE's makeshift office.

> JOE
>
> Now, look you're actually going to have to
> be me during these rehearsals, so I can
> watch the scenes.

> MOLLY
>
> Oh great. Thanks for the warning. So
> unlike you. So how does Herr Direktor
> rehearse his part?

> JOE
>
> We'll find time. And I'll nick all your
> best bits. I seem to remember that you
> were rather better than me during all
> those amateur dramatics.

> MOLLY
>
> Well yes, 'cos that's where I do it, as
> opposed to thinking someone might pay me
> to do it.

> JOE
>
> Yes, it's a horrible concept that, isn't
> it? It's caught me out before now.

> MOLLY
>
> But you still persist.

> JOE
>
> Just about. I think this is what we call
> the last gasp.

> MOLLY
>
> So why don't you make it easier on your-
> self this time by doing a comedy, or some-
> thing somebody might be interested to see?

> JOE
>
> Well, that's where you and me part company
> as always. I think if we can do it with
> humour, passion and reality people will be
> interested in seeing it. I saw this play
> when I was fifteen, and it changed my
> life. You don't forget that. I don't think
> I was any different then to any of your
> hormonally confused kids now. All I was
> ever interested in was girls and wanking.
> Unfortunately, hardly ever in that order.
> I saw this play and it spoke to my heart,
> and my head, and my chief reproductive
> organ.

(CONTINUED)

37   CONTINUED: 37

                              MOLLY
                Can that go in the programme notes?

     JOE throws a ball of paper at MOLLY.

                                                                 CUT.

38   INT. CHURCH - MORNING.   38

     FADGE is taking a warm-up session with the cast. A bizarre
     collection of trussed up, semi-lycraed wrecks. FADGE beats
     a drum and makes noises. The others sway, bend and stretch
     with varying degrees of commitment. It's like a scene from
     One Flew Over the Cuckoo's Nest.

                              FADGE
                Release that pain, get it out, throw it
                way, up and down, up and down, out of your
                head ... and now it becomes a ... train of
                fear ... a train of fear ... and vocalise
                ... poop poop ... poop poop ...

                                                                 CUT.

39   INT. CHURCH STAGE - DAY.   39

     CARNFORTH is giving us his Bernardo. Unconvincingly.
                              CARNFORTH
                'Who's there?'

     VERNON as Francisco is about to carry on. JOE leaps up on
     the stage. The rest of the company are sitting in the audi-
     torium.

                              JOE
                Great. Terrific. Huge potential there.

     JOE moves CARNFORTH to one side. CARNFORTH crashes his pike
     into the scenery.

                              CARNFORTH
                Sorry. Sorry.
                              JOE
                It's a bit limp.
                              CARNFORTH
                Limp?

                                                          (CONTINUED)

                              JOE

Well you know. He has seen a ghost and he
is probably expecting to see another one.
Listen, Hamlet is a tremendous ghost
story. I want to see that fear - I want to
smell that fear.

                         CARNFORTH

Oh, I see. I see. That's good. Fear.

                              JOE

Alright. Start again.

JOE goes back to his seat.

                         CARNFORTH

  'Who's there?'

No difference.

                              JOE

                    (running up to Carnforth)

No. No. No. It still doesn't convince me.
Now look let's take a little time out here
to ground this in some sort of reality.
You tell me, Carnforth, when was the last
time you were really terrified. Can you
remember when that was or if there was
such a time?

                         CARNFORTH

Um ... yes ... Yes I can remember, I was
on my way to have Sunday lunch with my
Mum. It was her birthday I remember
... bit of a 'do' ... you know. And I got
a flat tyre on the motorway and well it
was touch and go whether I would get there
on time and I was ... pretty terrified
then ... you know ...

                              JOE

And how did this terror manifest itself?

                         CARNFORTH

Well ... I probably took a little longer
to change the tyre than it would have
... hands shaking, that sort of thing.

                              JOE

Right. Look let's bring that situation
here. That fear.

                    (leaving the stage)

Alright, let's have another go.

39 CONTINUED: (2)   39

    JOE runs back to the auditorium. CARNFORTH starts again.
    This time miming changing a tyre.

                        CARNFORTH

            'Who's there?'

                        JOE

            No. No. No. You don't have to change the
            tyre.

                        CARNFORTH

            I'm so sorry. Sorry everybody. I thought
            you wanted ...

                                                    CUT.

40 EXT. CHURCHYARD - DAY.   40

    TOM massaging FADGE's hand strenuously. NINA sits with them
    munching on some celery.

                        TOM

            Tricky first morning.

                        NINA

            Yes, first scenes, they're always so
            difficult.

                        TOM

            I can feel the production in here already
            ... I can feel your pain.

                        FADGE

            Can you Tom?

                        TOM

            Relax.

    TOM gives one final agonising squeeze. FADGE shrieks.

                                                    CUT.

41 INT. STAGE - DAY.   41

    The first court scene. It has been going well. HENRY in
    full voice, very pleased with himself. TERRY in practice
    skirt and falsies.

                        HENRY

            ' ... But now my cousin Hamlet and my son'

                        MOLLY

            'A little more than kin and less than
            kind'

                                            (CONTINUED)

41 CONTINUED:

> HENRY
>
> 'How is it that the clouds still hang on
> you?'

> MOLLY
>
> 'Not so my lord, I am too much i' the sun'

TERRY begins in a put-on voice of throaty, grande-dame
theatricality.

> TERRY
>
> 'Good Hamlet, cast thy nighted colour off
> And let thine eye look like a friend on
> Denmark.'

HENRY stops.

> HENRY
>
> Is he going to do it like that?

> TERRY
>
> Like what, you rude girl?

> HENRY
>
> Like Larry the Lamb on speed.

> JOE
>
> Right, now let me just stop you both
> there. Henry, if you could leave the
> interruptions to me. Thank you. Terry,
> look I am slightly concerned about the
> voice. The general movement fine but the
> voice is just a little ...

> TERRY
>
> But it's what they all do darling. All the
> grande dames. They don't talk like they do
> in the real world. They put on the old
> cigarette gravel. The tragic trill. The
> emotional break in the middle of the line,
> the operatic cadenzas, ... I'm not making
> it up, they do.

> JOE
>
> Sure and sometimes it's very good, and
> sometimes they're very wrong and give
> Shakespeare a bad name. Technically it's
> brilliant ... but you don't sound like a
> ... human being.

> HENRY
>
> More like a robot with piles.

> JOE
>
> That's not what I meant.

(CONTINUED)

41   CONTINUED: (2)   41

                              TERRY

          Look that's what I hear love when I go to
          the classical theatre. I thought that's
          what you did.

                              JOE

          Have a little think about something more
          natural. I think you'd do it brilliantly.
                    (leaving the stage)
          Alright, here we go.

     Beat.

                              NINA

          Actually, Terry, something to be aware of.
          Somebody told me about it. You must be
          very careful that you don't invert your
          opening line as Gertrude. Apparently it's
          quite a famous cock-up so that instead of
          saying 'Good Hamlet, cast thy nighted
          colour off' you can end up saying 'Good
          Hamlet cast off thy coloured nightie'.

     Embarrassed pause.

                              NINA (Cont'd)

          You probably won't do that yourself ... I
          just ... anyone like some tea?

                                                             CUT.

42   INT. JOE'S OFFICE - NIGHT.   42

     JOE in his makeshift office, sorting out papers. MOLLY
     arrives in full rage carrying a letter.

                              MOLLY

          Bloody Landlord!

                              JOE

          What?

                              MOLLY

          Well you know you paid the rent?

                              JOE

          Yeah, three weeks in advance.

                              MOLLY

          Well, he says he wants a week's rent out
          of that for unpaid electric bills that he
          says the school's liable for.

                                                      (CONTINUED)

42   CONTINUED:

                         JOE

Are you liable?

                         MOLLY

Of course not. He's chancing his arm.

                         JOE

Well, challenge it.

                         MOLLY

We will, but he's stalling, till after
Christmas.

                         JOE

Oh, can he do that?

                         MOLLY

Of course not. But he's a shit and he
already has your cash.

                         JOE

What does that mean?

                         MOLLY

Well, that as far as he's concerned he
wants another week's rent or he'll turf us
out.

                         JOE

Well we won't go.

                         MOLLY

Well if we do that he says he'll cut off
all the services, water, gas, electric.

                         JOE

Bloody hell, Moll.

                         MOLLY

I've spoken to the council. He's within
his rights. If us or the school doesn't
pay up, we contravene the terms of the
special performing licence.

                         JOE

Oh come on, we don't have time for that.

                         MOLLY

I didn't plan it, Joe.

                         JOE

When's his deadline?

                         MOLLY

End of the final week. Day before we open.

42 CONTINUED: (2)   42

                              JOE

          Or?

                              MOLLY

          He'll send his mates in to close us down.

                              JOE

          Christ, I don't have £700.

                              MOLLY

          Well neither do I.

                              JOE

          Alright, alright. We'll think of some-
          thing. Don't tell the actors.

     NINA comes into the office. She has her coat on. They
     switch into cheery mode.

                              NINA

          Sorry to interrupt. Just came to say well
          done. Both of you. Wonderful first day.
          You were so brave. It's all very exciting.

                              JOE

          Thanks very much Nina.

                              MOLLY

          Are you off out for the evening?

                              NINA

          Oh no. It's Tom's turn to cook. We're hav-
          ing vegetarian steak and kidney pudding. I
          wouldn't miss that for the world. I'm just
          off to the phone box. See you later.

                              MOLLY

          Who's she off to ring?

                              JOE

          Her husband.

                                                        CUT.

43   INT. CHURCH NOTICE BOARD - NIGHT.   43

     JOE is pinning the rehearsal call to the board. VERNON is
     putting something up on the wall.

                              VERNON

          Well boss, another day, another .00001 of
          a dollar. How was it for you?

                              JOE
Not without its moments Vernon.

VERNON reveals what he was hanging, a poster - Vernon's
name in massive type - VERNON SPATCH IS POLONIUS IN ...
                            VERNON
Not bad eh? Just a bit of fun.
                              JOE
No, no, it works well. A little under-
stated I fear.
                            VERNON
Well, it's worth it just to see Henry's
face. By the way boss, are you considering
having anyone come to see this thing?
                              JOE
First things first Vernon. We've got to
get the show right.
                            VERNON
But what about tickets, box-office, the
cash-advance, advertising?
                              JOE
That's all in hand. You know, they set up
a box-office at Molly's school and people
can book through her home number. Fadge
has agreed to do the catering and the
front of house etc. So we're geared up.
                            VERNON
And how many people are currently booked?
                              JOE
Well, you know figures can be a bit mis-
leading at this time of the year,
Christmas shopping etc.
                            VERNON
Has anyone booked?
                              JOE
We're looking at business mainly on the
night.
                            VERNON
No one's booked?
                              JOE
Not yet. No.

                                        CUT.

44 EXT. PHONE BOX - NIGHT.   44

We cut between JOE and MARGARETTA on the telephone. She is
at home, in bed, reading a script.

>   JOE
>
> I've got a bit of a cash flow problem with
> the landlord.

>   MARGARETTA
>
> Oh Joe, not again, you promised.

>   JOE
>
> Yeah, I'm just a bit stuck.

>   MARGARETTA
>
> Well unstick yourself darling. I'm sure
> you can reason with him.

>   JOE
>
> I don't think so. He's got some strong and
> very persuasive friends in the building
> trade.

>   MARGARETTA
>
> You'll think of something. And how's your
> Hamlet?

>   JOE
>
> Well a little underdone at the moment.
> Molly's mainly filling in for me, but
> she's rather good too the bitch.

>   MARGARETTA
>
> Don't undervalue yourself darling. I don't
> want to drag reluctant casting directors
> down there to see you being bad.

>   JOE
>
> No. Understood.

>   MARGARETTA
>
> Oh and darling, more dramas on the Dylan
> Judd front. Apparently she wants billing
> and a personal trainer. Contracts not
> signed, filming imminent. Oooh she's push-
> ing her luck.

>   JOE
>
> I do wish him well.

>   MARGARETTA
>
> I'll keep you posted. Are you feeling less
> suicidal now?

>   JOE
>
> I suppose so.

(CONTINUED)

44 CONTINUED: 44

MARGARETTA

Then it's working. Marvellous. Good night
sweet prince.

JOE

Goodnight.

CUT.

45   INT. CHURCH STAGE - DAY.   45

Rehearsals in progress. TOM, VERNON and NINA. The others
dotted around. VERNON is being very theatrical. TOM is
using an accent from another solar system. JOE watches
aghast.

VERNON

' ... and let him ply his music'

TOM

'Well my lord'

VERNON

'Farewell'

JOE
(to Vernon)

Hold on a sec. Um ... it's a bit ...

VERNON

Much?

JOE

Yes ... I don't know if the nose is going
to your head, if you'll pardon the expression, but I'm getting more Shylock than
Polonius.

VERNON

I like to be bold early on but I get the
message chief. It's basically L.C.A.

JOE

Um?

VERNON

Less Crap Acting.

JOE

That's about the size of it. Thank you.
Tom?

TOM

Yes, darling.

(CONTINUED)

                          JOE

Your accent.

                          TOM

Oh you noticed it.

                          JOE

I think you'd have to be from Pluto not to
notice it.

                          TOM

Good, good.

                          JOE

Unfortunately, I think you also have to
come from Pluto to understand it.

                          TOM
                    (bridling)
It has to be different darling. I am playing lots of roles, however small some of
them are now. I want each one to be dis-
tinct. I've taken my cue from his name:
Reynaldo - you know, Reynard - sort of
foxy you know, hence the accent.

                          JOE

A foxy accent?

                          TOM

Well, you see, I asked myself how would a
fox speak. Rather covert, rather secretive.

                          JOE

I'm getting more Russian than secretive or
foxy.

                          TOM

Let me work on it.

                          JOE

Alright, thank you. OK, here we go then.

                          NINA

Joe, before we do my entrance, I wondered
if I could try something?

                          JOE

Yes, certainly Nina.

                          NINA

I was thinking, bearing in mind what you
were saying to Carnforth the other day.
You know, about fear and everything and I

                    (MORE)

45   CONTINUED: (2)   45

                         NINA (Cont'd)
        was sort of thinking for this scene that
        she really ought to be genuinely scared to
        bits.

                         JOE
        Exactly.

                         NINA
        I mean, almost violent, hysterical, just
        preparing the audience slightly for later
        on when she goes mad, and so that we can
        really see the effect Hamlet has on her.
        The effect of seeing his flesh, the sexual
        threat, you know, just very much 'out of
        control' almost ...

                         JOE
        Excellent. Right. You try it. Listen, in
        your own time.

They begin the scene again. VERNON is more natural. TOM is
less Russian.

                         VERNON
        'Goodbye ye, fare ye well.'

                         TOM
        'Good my lord'

                         VERNON
        'And let him ply his music'

                         TOM
        'Well, my lord'

                         VERNON
        'Farewell'

At this point with a great scream NINA rushes from the back
of the church. She is possessed by the role. She is also
blind.

                         NINA
        'Oh my lord I have been so affrighted.'

VERNON holds open his arms. She runs past him, off the edge
of the steps, and lands, everything akimbo, face down on
the floor with a great thud..

46 INT. CHURCH - DAY.   46

In the background JOE and TOM are performing primitive
first aid on NINA, while VERNON films. In foreground FADGE
is sewing a costume, CARNFORTH is filling in his crossword.

                    FADGE

If that girl makes it to the first night
without serious accident, I'll be amazed.

                    CARNFORTH

I know, she does seem to have a bit of a
vision problem doesn't she.

                    FADGE

She's brushed her teeth with soap for the
last three nights. But she won't admit it.

                    CARNFORTH

Yes, she's a stubborn old thing under all
that dizzy stuff.

                    FADGE

But nice, very nice.

FADGE starts to pull apart the costume she's sewing.

                    FADGE

Oh buggering, buggery, bugger.

                    CARNFORTH

You alright?

                    FADGE

No ... it's these bloody costumes - I've
brought every period with me but I can't
quite decide and it's getting a bit ...

                    CARNFORTH

Late in the day?

                    FADGE

Don't say that for God's sake.

Beat.

You're very impressive with that crossword.

                    CARNFORTH

Well, you know what the secret is? I don't
answer any of the clues.

                    FADGE

What do you mean?

                                            (CONTINUED)

46 CONTINUED: 46

> CARNFORTH
>
> I just take my time and fill in all the
> empty boxes. Any old letters will do. I've
> always been terrible at the bloody things.
> But it takes my mind off the God awful
> business of acting.
>
> FADGE
>
> Is your name really Carnforth Greville?
>
> CARNFORTH
>
> No, it's Keith Branch. I just pinched one
> that I thought had the requisite amount of
> mystery and glamour.
>
> FADGE
>
> What did your parents think?
>
> CARNFORTH
>
> They were rather disappointed actually.
> Well, they'd done a lot of scrimping to
> put me through drama school and whatnot.
> Well, they really believed in me. Mum
> especially. I don't think I've dealt with
> parental expectation terribly well. What
> about you? Were you christened Fadge?
>
> FADGE
>
> Hardly. I was christened Mildred. Not the
> name to have if you seek distinction as a
> designer, which I rather pitifully did.
> But I was adopted you see, so I didn't
> think it really mattered.
>
> CARNFORTH
>
> I think it's rather sweet.
>
> FADGE
>
> Thank you Keith.
>
> CARNFORTH
>
> My pleasure, Mildred.

FADGE looks around the church.

> FADGE
>
> It's rather fun all this sometimes isn't
> it?
>
> CARNFORTH
>
> It is rather. Ooo, I've just got another
> clue.

                                                        CUT.

47   EXT. PICTURESQUE CHURCH BENCH - DAY.   47

NINA sits with sandwich in hand and bandage on head, dis-
consolate. JOE offers her some tea from his vacuum flask.

                    JOE

So why, no glasses ah? Or ... I don't
know ...

                    NINA

I don't know either. I don't want to see
the world in sharp focus.

                    JOE

Why?

                    NINA

Because it's horrible.

                    JOE

Do you really think so? You're always so
amazingly positive and bright.

                    NINA

And dizzy?

                    JOE

No, I didn't say that.

                    NINA

That's what Dad says on the phone every
night. He thinks this whole thing of being
an actress and working in the theatre is
just a terrible passing phase.

                    JOE

I'm sure he's very proud really.

                    NINA

I hoped he would be if he came to see it.
It was my first proper part.

                    JOE

Still I expect your husband gives you his
support?

                    NINA

Yeah, he does in his way.

                    JOE

I'm sorry ... does he live very far away?

                    NINA

He's dead. It's alright. It's just one of
those things. One of those ghastly, bloody
awful things.

(CONTINUED)

47 CONTINUED: 47

                          JOE

Was he ill?

                          NINA

No, it was much more stupid and absurd
than that. He was a fighter pilot, really.
A great dancer and a very good fighter
pilot. But he crashed. A mid-air collision
at tremendous speed. A one in a million
chance. In the lake district. It was a
beautiful day. But then I suppose it usu-
ally is. Not that it makes it any easier.

                          JOE

How old was he?

                          NINA

Thirty-three. Christ died at thirty-three.
Rather more painfully I suppose.

                          JOE

What did you do when it happened?

                          NINA

Went to pieces. The usual. And then after
a while you start to put life back together again. Martin always used to say
that 'Life is a silly old business - you
fall down, you get up, you fall down, you
get up.' Literally in my case.

                          JOE

And had you always been in the theatre?

                          NINA

Oh no, always in the services. Service
family. R.A.F. Of course. Theatre was all
a lot of nonsense, spare time stuff if you
had to. Martin was different though. He
always believed I could be a grown-up
actress.

                          JOE

I think you're a very grown-up actress.

                                              CUT.

48   INT. CHURCH - DAY.   48

  Rehearsal montage. HENRY in full dramatic flow as Claudius.

48   CONTINUED: 48

> HENRY
>
> 'Oh, my offence is rank.' (He sinks dra-
> matically to his knees with great speed.
> Mistake.) Ah! Can we rehearse on something
> harder?

Beat on JOE's reaction.

                                                              CUT.

NINA in moustache, beard and glasses as an attendant, is
acting with TERRY as the Queen. The moustache flaps up and
down as she speaks.

> TERRY
>
> 'So full of artless jealousy is guilt,
> It spills itself in fearing to be spilt.
> Sin siling to be fitt,'
>
> Oh God, if I go through that sentence
> again I'll lose a filling.

                                                              CUT.

CLOSE-UP on JOE's weary face as we hear the sounds of the
play off-screen.

                                                              CUT.

VERNON and MOLLY in the closet scene. MOLLY is in the act
of killing VERNON, who is hidden behind a screen.

> MOLLY
>
> 'Dead, dead for a ducat, dead.'

After a series of strangulated 'aaagh's' VERNON emerges
with a comedy half-sword wired around his head.

> VERNON
>
> Where would you like it love, when I stag-
> ger out dramatically from behind the
> arras? It could be anywhere with Hamlet.
> At this stage he hardly knows his arras
> from his elbow.
>
> VERNON AND MOLLY
>
> Ho, ho.

                                                              CUT.

CLOSE-UP on TOM as Fortinbras. TOM has become Norwegian. He
talks strangely.

                                                         (CONTINUED)

48   CONTINUED: (2)   48

                         TOM/FORTINBRAS
          'Go, Captain, from me greet the Danish
          King.
          Tell him that by his licence Fortinbras
          Craves the conveyance of a promis'd march
          Over his kingdom. You know the ren-
          dezvous.'

                         JOE
          Tom, I just ... don't get it ...

                         TOM
          Norwegian, darling Norwegian ... all those
          fiords and roll mop herrings, they walk
          differently. They talk differently.

                         JOE
          Yes, but they do live on planet Earth.

                         TOM
          This isn't easy Joe.

                                                          CUT.

     FADGE is taking CARNFORTH through the special movement
     required to play both Rosencrantz and Guildenstern at the
     same time. It involves constant rotation, but with exagger-
     ated movements, like Marcel Marceau after a few pints.

                         FADGE
          And Guildenstern and Rosencrantz and
          Guildenstern and Rosencrantz (she turns)
          'My honoured lord' (She turns again, a
          different voice.) 'My most dear Lord.'

                         JOE
          What have I done.

                                                          CUT.

49   INT. CHURCH - DAY.   49

     The company gathered. Rather gloomily listening to JOE's
     summing up.

                         JOE
          Well ... that was an extraordinary first
          week. No one said it would be easy. It's a
          big play. And we've covered every scene
          ...

                         HENRY
                    (under his breath)
          In shit.

                                                    (CONTINUED)

49 CONTINUED: 49

                              JOE

          And that in itself is a great achievement
          ... I think we have to worry a little less
          about the exterior of these characters;
          clothes and walks and accents, etc., and
          concentrate a little more on each
          individual's needs, their drives. What is
          it they want and need? Why they do what
          they do. Not How. The How will take care
          of itself if we ask always, why, why, why?

                            HENRY

          Believe me darling, I've been asking.

                              JOE

          If we can use that energy, that hunger,
          the very hunger that's brought us here for
          this unique opportunity, I think you'll
          find that the play will give you back a
          great deal. You have to trust yourselves
          ... We have to trust ourselves. We have a
          great deal to offer ... both to each other
          ... and to the audiences ... and do remem-
          ber please, it is only the end of the
          first week.

                            HENRY

          Yes, the problem is love, there is no sec-
          ond week. We have four more days before
          the technical rehearsal. One dress
          rehearsal on Christmas Eve afternoon, and
          one in the evening ...

     Beat.

                              JOE

          We have set ourselves a challenge there is
          no doubt. But at Shakespeare's own the-
          atre, a six-week season would have pro-
          duced thirty-five performances of seven-
          teen different plays including at times
          four world premieres, so as Polonius says
          'Sometimes Brevity can be the soul of
          wit'. But I don't think we should lose our
          nerve.

                                                    CUT.

50   INT. HENRY and TERRY'S BEDROOM - EVENING.   50

     HENRY and TERRY's dorm. Two camp beds (ooo er, vicar) quite
     close together, copies of the play on their laps.

                                                      (CONTINUED)

50 CONTINUED: 50

                         TERRY

It's bloody difficult isn't it, old Sally
Shakespeare? Especially for us new girls.

                         HENRY

Join the club love.

                         TERRY

But you've done it before.

                         HENRY

Never. Just seems that way.

                         TERRY

Ooo you minx. You're full of surprises.

                         HENRY

I know, love, just an old bullshitter.
Always wanted to do the classics, of
course. Used to read about the old
Shakespeare Companies. You know, eight
plays in six days. Travelling from town to
town on a Sunday. Hundreds of people wav-
ing the actors off from the platform. So
romantic. Unfortunately I was born out of
my time. When I joined the business all
that was gone. It was divided in two.
There was the 'proper' theatre, you know
Stratford and all that, and then there was
the commercial stuff. Well, a little sub-
urban oik like me, had no chance of the
tights and fluffy white shirts. I was
straight into understudying old men and
'anyone for tennis?'

                         TERRY

So you haven't really done any
Shakespeare?

                         HENRY

No.

                         TERRY

You must be a bit nervous.

                         HENRY

Total brown-trouser job love. But you
can't show the young ones your fear. So
you cover up by being a crabby old git.

                         TERRY

Oh, you're very convincing.

50   CONTINUED: (2)   50

                              HENRY

          Well we all have our crosses to bear. Mind
          you, you know, I do feel as though I've
          done it before, the classics. Through
          people like Irving and Tree.

                              TERRY

          I adore Irving.

                              HENRY

          Do you know about him?

                              TERRY

          Darling, just 'cos I'm in a frock at the
          end of a pier, doesn't mean I don't have
          a grasp of theatrical history.

                              HENRY

          He was amazing, wasn't he? Oik, just like
          me, a stammer, a limp, every disadvantage
          and yet the first actor ever to be
          knighted.

                              TERRY

          And he died with his boots on.

                              HENRY

          That's right, in harness. On tour, in
          Bradford. What a way to go. (Beat.) Mind
          you I've died in Bradford a few times.

51   INT. JOE'S OFFICE - NIGHT.   51

     We don't know where we are to begin with. It seems like
     another rehearsal scene. A close-up of acting with utter
     conviction.

                              JOE

          'O God, O God,
          How weary, stale, flat, and unprofitable
          Seem to me all the uses of this world!'

     MOLLY leans into frame.

                              MOLLY

          That's not bad, Sir Laurence.

                              JOE

          Well, understand how he feels, Vivien.

     He's sitting over a page of accounts.

(CONTINUED)

51 CONTINUED: 51

                              JOE

          Oh Christ, what are we gonna do? This was
          all so carefully worked out. Based on a
          (let's face it) optimistic turnout of
          three hundred people a night for seven
          performances making an average donation
          ... of -

                             MOLLY

          Donation?

                              JOE

          Well, we can't charge proper ticket
          prices, that's not what it's about, any-
          way, an average donation of £2.50, that is
          £750 per night, which makes it £5,250 for
          the run, less £2100 for the production
          budget and rent, less £100 per week per
          person profit-share (hopefully)for three
          weeks for eight people, less £150 for the
          first night drinks and Christmas dinner,
          less £600 for food and utilities. Anyway,
          brings it all back to nothing. It cer-
          tainly doesn't magic up £700 for produc-
          tion week rent, and in any case, that's
          based on the idea of a box-office advance
          cash from which I could borrow money, as
          opposed to my credit card, which is now
          kaput.

VERNON has been listening.

                            VERNON

          Spatch to the rescue chief. (Vernon is
          wearing a sandwich board advertising the
          production. He's also carrying leaflets.)
          Fadge did the board. I ran off the flyers
          on my computer. I'm going to trail the
          streets of Hope. If you give me the tick-
          ets, I'll sell some 'live'.

                          JOE/MOLLY

          Fantastic.

MOLLY hands him a book of cloakroom tickets with dates
handwritten across them and a little cash bag.

                            VERNON

          I also have a booking at Chelford Castle.

                              JOE

          What, the ruin?

                                              (CONTINUED)

51   CONTINUED: (2)   51

                              VERNON
        Part ruin, part Country Hotel.
                              MOLLY
                        (to Joe)
        After your time love. The beginning of the
        attempted yuppification of the area. A
        smooth blend of ancient monument and
        leisure facility. Didn't work.
                              VERNON
        Ah, but the hotel does. For Christmas any-
        way. It's fully booked and they are about
        to get my occasional cabaret act, of
        crooning and conjuring.
                              JOE
        And might you sell some tickets for
        Hamlet?
                              VERNON
        Or my middle name's not 'fabulously tal-
        ented and modest'.
                              JOE
        Vernon, I love you. In a platonic way,
        obviously.
                              MOLLY
        Obviously.
                              JOE
        Although you do have a lovely ass.

                                                        CUT.

52   INT. CHURCH - DAY.   52

     JOE, now playing Hamlet, with some fire, and TERRY in the
     Closet Scene.

                              TERRY
        'This is the very coinage of your brain.
        This bodiless creation ecstasy is very
        cunning in.'
                              JOE
        'Ecstasy!
        My pulse as yours doth temperately keep
        time,
        And makes as healthful music. It is not
        madness
                        (MORE)

(CONTINUED)

52 CONTINUED: 52

                          JOE (Cont'd)

That I have uttered ... Mother, for love
of grace,
Lay not that flattering unction to your
soul,
That not your trepass but my madness
speaks
It will but skin and film the ulcerous
place,
Whiles rank corruption, mining all within,
Infects unseen. Confess yourself to
heaven,
Repent what's past, avoid what is to
come.'

                          TERRY

'Oh, Hamlet thou hast cleft my heart in
twain' -

I'm sorry I can't go on.

                          JOE

          (excited)

It's terrific. It's terrific. You must,
you must. You're just avoiding confronting
it as an actor that's all, that's all, you
have to feel her guilt, you have to confess to your son -

                          TERRY

I tried, I tried ... he wouldn't listen.

TERRY bursts into tears and runs from the rehearsal.

                          JOE

... what ... ?

                          VERNON

Bit close to home love.

                                                    CUT.

53 INT. CHURCH BY STAINED WINDOW - DAY.   53

HENRY listening quietly to TERRY.

                          HENRY

When?

                          TERRY

When I was seventeen. The only time I'd
ever been with a girl. Before or since.

                                        (CONTINUED)

53 CONTINUED: 53

                          HENRY
                    (amazed)
Just once?

                          TERRY
I know, bull's eye. This girl wasn't firing blanks.

                          HENRY
What did you do?

                          TERRY
Well, I was already half way to running
off to the circus if you know what I mean.
She was determined to have the kid. Not
that I'd have known what to have done even
if she hadn't been. Once she found out
that I kicked with the other foot she'd
have nothing to do with me anyway.

                          HENRY
Do you know where they are?

                          TERRY
Oh. He found me love. Kids do. They get a
bee in their bonnet. All turn into
Sherlock Holmes when it comes to their
real Mummy and Daddy. Christmas Eve,
Bradford as it happens, *Puss 'n Boots*,
four years ago.

                          HENRY
What happened?

                          TERRY
Well, it was a bit like that scene we just
did. Not quite such a good script. I'd
abandoned him and his mother (who he hates
for hiding me). He was ashamed of my job
and what I was. Am. And never wanted to
see me again. No surprises.

                          HENRY
He must have been very upset.

                          TERRY
So was I.

                          HENRY
Have you seen him since?

                          TERRY
Oh, I've written to him. I get the occa-
sional card. The thing is, Henry, this
play brings it back more than I thought
                    (MORE)

                                              (CONTINUED)

53   CONTINUED: (2)   53

                              TERRY (Cont'd)

          possible. Shakespeare wasn't stupid.
          Families you know, they don't work do
          they?

                              HENRY

          I don't know love. I've never had one,
          always fancied one but it never worked
          out ...

                              TERRY

          I'll never be able to go on.

                              HENRY

          Yes you will. We both will.

                                                        CUT.

54   INT. CHURCH - NIGHT.   54

     Everyone tired.

                              TOM

          'Thought and affliction, passion, hell
          itself
          She turns to favour ... '

     CARNFORTH staggering in.

                              CARNFORTH

                    (interrupting)

          Has anyone seen a bottle of lemonade I had
          with me? I've got a bit of a sore throat.

                              VERNON

          Lemonade?

                              CARNFORTH

          Yes, lemonade. What's your problem buster?

                              JOE

          OK. OK, let's go again from Ophelia's song
          and please, please give this scene the
          intensity it deserves. You're all shying
          away from the power of this play. Now this
          scene is about loss. The loss of sense,
          Ophelia's madness, the loss of a sister,
          the loss of a relationship between
          Claudius and Gertrude, and crucially
          the loss, the death of someone they have
          all in their own ways experienced a pro-
          found love for, that's a human emotion we

                              (MORE)

                                              (CONTINUED)

54   CONTINUED: 54

                         JOE (Cont'd)
          can all share - that's where we connect
          with the audience in Hope or wherever, we
          have to believe you have suffered such a
          loss - (He starts to realise.) I'm sorry
          Nina -

                         NINA
          No, you're perfectly right Joe. We must
          imagine the reality of it. I'm fine.

                         JOE
          Alright. Let's go again from that point.

The atmosphere changes as the tired company register the
heartbreaking effort with which NINA starts to sing the
song. A voice of such fragility and simplicity. A beautiful
tune, an achingly painful moment.

                         NINA
                       (slowly)
          'And will he not come again?
          And will he not come again?
          No, no, he is dead,
          Go to thy death bed,
          He never will come again.'
          Sorry.

She runs off distraught.

                         TOM
                       (quietly)
          'Do you see this, Oh God.'

JOE drops his head. Silence.

                                                    CUT.

55   EXT. PHONE BOX - NIGHT.   55

We cut between JOE and MARGARETTA on the telephone. She is
at home decorating her Christmas Tree.

                         MARGARETTA
          Look darling, if I start now it will be an
          open drain. You've made ridiculously opti-
          mistic calculations based on an income
          that simply doesn't exist.

                                                  (CONTINUED)

55 CONTINUED: 55

JOE

It will.

MARGARETTA

Well, when it does, I will forward some
cash ...

JOE

Have you anything exciting to tell me?

MARGARETTA

Well, it looks like Dylan's blown it, darling. They start shooting in LA on Boxing
Day and she hasn't even had a costume fit-
ting yet. The producer, Nancy Crawford,
herself no less is in town recce-ing for-
eign locations - she is going mad.

JOE

Can't you just get me a week of his
expenses?

MARGARETTA

Darling, you're under too much pressure.
Why don't you take Sunday off and relax.
Remember it's Christmas. You could write
to Santa.

JOE, mourning, leaves the phone box and walks slowly with
his head held down, up the country lane.

                                                          CUT.

56 INT. CHURCH STAGE - EVENING.   56

TOM as Fortinbras. CARNFORTH as the Captain, now almost
totally insensible.

JOE

Let's start again.

TOM

'Go, Captain, from me greet the Danish
King -'

Suddenly CARNFORTH burps. TOM stops in mid-sentence.
Fatigue has got the better of him. The tantrum begins.

TOM
(yelling)

Sorry. I'm sorry I can't do this, darling
(MORE)

                                                      (CONTINUED)

56 CONTINUED: 56

                         TOM (Cont'd)

          - it's just not possible. I'm playing
          four hundred parts, you won't allow me to
          do a single accent, I've got a Captain
          here who can't walk in a straight line.

                         CARNFORTH

     Hey, steady on ...

                         TOM

     If you could do that love, we'd be fine
     ... Joe ... I'm committed to this project
     132%, you know that. Everything that I am
     as a human being is here. I bring it in
     every morning, it's yours. My energy is
     always positive energy, physically, intel-
     lectually and ... thing me. But all I ever
     get back from people is ridicule. Let's
     all have a cheap joke at Tom's expense,
     well that's fine that really is perfectly
     all right, because my shoulders are broad.
     I ... em ... I've kept my own peace. . . . I
     haven't rung my agent.

                         VERNON

     She hasn't got an agent.

                         TOM

     Yes I have. . . . Shut up. Shut up, will you
     ... It really isn't fair ... It's just too
     ... too much.

Silence.

                         JOE

                    (weary)

     I'm sorry Tom. Very sorry.

TOM breathes deeply.

                         TOM

     I'm sorry too Joe. I'm sorry everyone.

                         HENRY

     Fine.

                         TOM

     Vernon, please.

                         JOE

     Start again.

TOM goes and hugs CARNFORTH.

                                              (CONTINUED)

56   CONTINUED: (2)   56

                              TOM
            Love this man.

TOM prepares, comes back on and starts to speak. CARNFORTH
holding on for grim death.

                              TOM
            'Go, Captain, from me -' (Vernon has
            started filming. Tantrum man re-emerges.)
            You see, it's hopeless. Absolutely hope-
            less. Everything we do, from wiping our
            ass to fluffing our lines has to be on
            camera. Can't we work in private for once?
            Why does everyone have to see behind the
            scenes, these days? Whatever happened to
            all the bloody mystery?

                            VERNON
                       (enraged, snaps)
            I'm recording our history love. It was
            discussed, right Joe. I think it's the
            least I deserve. I'm the only one who's
            got off his ass to sell this show.

                              TOM
            Always vulgar.

                            VERNON
            Don't you want anyone to see it? Or would
            you rather just do your bloody stupid
            accents in front of the mirror?

JOE cuts across the row emerging. He is now officially at
the end of his tether. Temper volcano.

                              JOE
            Right, that's it, that's it, that's it.
            That is it. That. Is. It.

Silence.

                              TOM
            What do you mean?

                              JOE
                         (yelling)
            I mean, the play's over. Finito, walk
            away. End of story. Kaput. Cheerio.

                            VERNON
            Do you really mean that?

                                                      (CONTINUED)

56 CONTINUED: (3)   56

>   JOE
>
> What is the point? What is the fucking
> point? I ... look. You're a perfectly
> decent bunch of people. A group of actors
> with all the normal insecurities and vani-
> ties. But basically I know you want to be
> here, we all want to do what's best for
> the show, but look at us? We argue. We're
> depressed. We've set ourselves too great a
> target. It is too personal for us all.
> It's a big play and we keep running up
> against it and hurting ourselves, and I
> for one can no longer know what I'm doing
> or why I'm doing it. I don't know this.
>
>   NINA
>
> That's not true.
>
>   JOE
>
>   (even bleaker)
>
> The miserable facts are we've run out of
> time to rehearse this, we have no audi-
> ence, we have no design. I'm sorry Fadge
> but that's true, and because I do not have
> the money to pay for it, we do not even
> have this venue for the run of the show.
> This whole idea, oh God, I see it now, no
> offence Molly, it's just pointless.
> Churches close and theatres close every
> week because finally people don't want
> them. The Hope *Hamlet* is a loser, led by
> the chief loser, yours truly, and circum-
> stances just force me to ask myself, not
> only what is the point of carrying on this
> meaningless shambles, but as the Yuletide
> season takes us in its grip I ask myself
> what is the point in going on with this
> miserable tormented life? I mean can any-
> one tell me, please, please, what makes
> this fucking life worth living?

Long silence. They are stunned. Eventually.

>   TOM
>
> I think you're just projecting negativity
> and I think it's really unfair on Fadge.
>
>   FADGE
>
> It's alright Tom.

Beat.

56 CONTINUED: (4)   56

                              VERNON

Rachmaninov.

                               JOE

What?

                              VERNON

That bit in *Brief Encounter*. And *Brief
Encounter* actually. That makes life worth
living. I'll buy you the video for Xmas.

Beat.

                              TERRY

Thinking of Tim being happy.

                              VERNON

Who's Tim?

                              TERRY

My son.

Beat.

                            CARNFORTH

Oh shit. Do we all have to do one?

                              VERNON

Shut up Carnforth.

Beat.

                              HENRY

Look. Joe, I might be speaking out of turn
but I feel, I think we all feel, that
... well some of what you say is true but
... we've come such a long way ... it's
certainly worth one more go ... Why don't
we call it a night and have one run at the
play tomorrow morning. At least do that
... eh ... ? Just for us ... eh ... boss?

JOE nods. They are still very quiet. MOLLY lets out a little sound.

                               JOE

What is it Moll?

                              MOLLY
                         (lip trembling)

You. You're my brother. You make life

                             (MORE)

                                                              (CONTINUED)

56 CONTINUED: (5)   56

MOLLY (Cont'd)

worth living. You make my life worth living. So don't say it's not -
(she breaks down)

He rushes to her. Hugs her ...

CUT.

57 INT. CHURCH - DAY.   57

Final Run Montage. Assorted scenes. CARNFORTH starts it
off, scaring them all shitless with:

CARNFORTH

'Who's there?'

Noël Coward lyrics burst into song.

CUT.

HENRY in stirring, stern form as Claudius.

HENRY

'And we beseech you, bend you to remain
Here in the cheer and comfort of our eye,
Our chiefest courtier, cousin and our
son.'

CUT.

Close-ups of the intense fascinated faces of the watching
company. It's all starting to happen!

CUT.

JOE in inspiring form, chills his audience.

JOE

'Bloody, bawdy villain!
Remorseless, treacherous, lecherous, kind-
less villain,
O Vengeance!'

CUT.

NINA, tragic, real.

(CONTINUED)

57 CONTINUED: 57

                              NINA
        'O, what a noble mind is here o'erthrown.'

                                                                    CUT.

TOM and CARNFORTH sober-ish and steady.

                              TOM
        ' ... and let him know so.'
                           CARNFORTH
        'I will do't my Lord.'
                              TOM
        'Go softly on.'

CARNFORTH hesitates for a moment over which way to go
softly, then makes a definite decision. He is wrong.

                           CARNFORTH
        Oh shit. Sorry.

FADGE gets up and leads him off.

                                                                    CUT.

                             TERRY
        ' ... but long it could not be.
        Till that her garments, heavy with their
        drink,
        Pulled the poor wretch from her melodious
        lay
        To muddy death.'

                                                                    CUT.

Wide Shot of the dead bodies. Last scene.

                              TOM
        'Go bid the soldiers shoot!'

A beat, and then tremendous applause from MOLLY and FADGE.
JOE leaps up. Everyone starts applauding and cheering.

                              JOE
                  (running to Molly and hugging her)
        That was terrific ... it really started to
        come alive ... I'm so proud of you all ...

                                                          (CONTINUED)

                              FADGE
                         (overexcited)
I'm nearly there Joe, nearly there. I
haven't quite hit on the right era yet.
We'll try things out during the tech but I
can feel it in my nips.

                              TOM
               (rushing up and hugging Joe)
Joe, do you realise how good you are in
this? You are so bloody good.

                              NINA
You were fantastic.

                              JOE
Oh ...

                              TERRY
But enough about me, darling, what did you
think of my performance ...

                              JOE
No ... everybody ... It was just ...every-
thing I could have hoped to see start
happening ... I just wish ...

                              VERNON
                         (hushing everyone)
Now ... Joe ... before you say anything.
We've talked to Moll about the financial
situation and we feel, the company feels
that we should help out. So anyway, we've
had a whip round. Everybody's put in what
they can, which I'm afraid isn't nearly
enough but ...

                              TOM
Fadge has sold her van.

                              JOE
Sold the van ... ? But you keep everything
in there, all your lights and costumes and
props ...

                              FADGE
They'll hold on to it till the new year.
If the play succeeds I'll buy it back.

                              JOE
Oh folks ... You mean ... ?

                              MOLLY
We paid it this morning Joe. The show can
go on.

                                        (CONTINUED)

57   CONTINUED: (3)   57

Beat. They all look at him.

>   JOE
> I don't know what to say. I'm ... I'm ...
>   HENRY
> A talentless git?
>   JOE
> Oh yes, certainly but ... thank you. Thank
> you very much. I think I'm going to cry.
>   NINA
> Don't do that. We all have a job to do.
> The technical rehearsal is first thing
> tomorrow morning. And Fadge has got half
> of us working on lights and blacking out
> the windows and the rest of us are going
> into Hope this afternoon to find our audi-
> ence.
>   JOE
> That's fantastic.
>   TOM
> But first we have a drink.

Loud cheers especially from CARNFORTH.

>   TERRY
> And some music!

Caption white on black:

                    ACT III
           'ANOTHER OPENING, ANOTHER SHOW!'

58   INT. CHURCH - DAY.   58

The place blacked-out as it will be for the evening perfor-
mances. All we can see is smoke swirling around, and hear
the noise of coughing. Eventually a bewildered CARNFORTH
comes into view. He can't see a thing.

>   CARNFORTH
> 'Who's there?'

58   CONTINUED: 58

JOE O/S

(from the auditorium)

No, no, remember Carnforth as we discov-
ered in rehearsal -

CARNFORTH

No I mean, who's there? - I can't see a
thing.

JOE

Oh, sorry Carnforth. Hey, well done
though, I really believed you the second
time there ... Vernon ... ?

VERNON emerges from the mist with a gong in hand.

VERNON

Yes, love?

JOE O/S

A little more definite with the gong. It
really sets up the tone of the play.

VERNON

Well it would help, if there wasn't quite
so much smoke back here. I keep thinking
I'm going to bump into Jack the Ripper,
and he's going to think I'm the man from
the Rank logo.

JOE

Well, can't one of the others do the gong?

VERNON

Well, Nina's blind enough as it is without
having to hit a gong in the mist,
Carnforth's on, Tom's on in a sec, you're
out there -

JOE

Well, what about Terry or Henry?

CUT.

59   INT. DRESSING ROOM - DAY.   59

(BLACKOUT)

TERRY and HENRY each at his dressing place. Mirrors and
desks already crammed with things. TERRY's face makes a
Robert Helpmann make-up look underdone. HENRY has gone for
rouge and a juve wig. They both look grotesque, and they've
hardly begun.

(CONTINUED)

59   CONTINUED: 59

                              TERRY
                 You look wonderful.

                              HENRY
                 You look gorgeous.

         They both laugh.

                                                        CUT.

60   INT. CHURCH - DAY.   60
                         (BLACKOUT)

         Trestle table and chairs in the auditorium. Pads of paper,
         primitive lighting console, behind which MOLLY sits making
         notes for JOE, whose face is lit dramatically by an angle-
         poise lamp.

                              JOE
                 Fadge?

         Out of the gloom with a miner's helmet and fluorescent
         jacket emerges FADGE holding a box/gun from which smoke is
         issuing.

                              FADGE
                 Teething problems, darling, that's why we
                 rehearse.

                              JOE
                 Yes, sure no problem with that Fadge. It's
                 just that we have spent all morning on
                 this and still haven't got beyond, 'Who's
                 there?' a question I fear many of the
                 audience will be asking, if the smoke's
                 this thick.

                              FADGE
                 Opening image, darling, it's crucial.

                              JOE
                 Understood. Any final decision about
                 props? Or costumes ... ?

                              FADGE
                 I've got till the end of the tech haven't
                 I?

                              JOE
                 Yes.

                                                        (CONTINUED)

60   CONTINUED: 60

FADGE

Let's remain open.

CUT.

61   INT. AUDITORIUM - AFTERNOON. (BLACKOUT)   61

Later that same day. MOLLY and JOE at their console.

JOE

Alright then let's go from the last line
of the previous scene, ready to bring on
the throne. Tom, give us your last line,
you can say it from off-stage for now.
Stand by LX and stand by sound. And
... Cue Tom.

TOM O/S

'Let's do't, I pray, and I this morning
know where we shall find him most conve-
nient.'

JOE

Go LX, Go Music ...

(They go.)

... that's good ... Vernon on first that's
right, check out the audience as if seeing
our imaginary court, excellent. Very good
to hold her hand ... Keep her out of trou-
ble, that's good ... and now the King and
Qu -

He stops in mid-sentence to take in what has appeared.
TERRY and HENRY look like something from the Lyceum circa
1885. Both think their characters are twenty-three years
old. Both are unsuccessfully trying to prove this.

TERRY

What you think darling?

HENRY

Not bad eh?

JOE

OK. Just ... Let's just hold it there
... erm do you know this is not a bad time
to have an informal chat about costume and
make-up ... Let's break for tea there,
back in an hour ... Um ... Henry and Terry
... a little word in your ear.

(CONTINUED)

61   CONTINUED: 61

                              HENRY

          What's wrong with him?

                              TERRY

          Don't know love, this is as good as it
          fucking gets.

                              HENRY

          If he don't like this, he don't like any-
          thing.

                              TERRY

          Fuck her, darling.

CARNFORTH appears at JOE's side.

                              CARNFORTH

          Joe, could you call your agent.

                              JOE

          What? I'll be right with you.

                              CARNFORTH

          I just popped down to the post office, And
          the landlord said there was a message for
          you to call your agent.

                              JOE

          The landlord? At the post office.

                              CARNFORTH

          Yes, it's a technical term, I believe
          ... came in with privatisation ... anyway
          ... urgent

                              JOE

          Wait a minute, its the day before
          Christmas eve, there are no agents work-
          ing.

                              CARNFORTH

          Oh yes, that's it, could you call her at
          home. Is there a message ... ? I could
          always pop back and have another ...

                              JOE

          I think you should work on your rotational
          movement exercises.

Beat.

                              CARNFORTH

          Don't drink. You don't need to.

                                                          CUT.

62   INT. CHURCH - TEA-TIME.   62

The entrance hall area. VERNON and MOLLY sit at a table
with the seating plan for the first night and tickets. In
the background FADGE and CARNFORTH are practising his rota-
tional exercises.

                        VERNON

So, how many does that make?

                        MOLLY

Well,I've got a party of ten kids from the
school coming down. £3 a head. Most of
them will have a bloody miserable
Christmas anyway.

                        VERNON

What, so you mean so even this pile of old
toss is better than nothing?

                        MOLLY

NO! But ...

                        VERNON

Only teasing.

             (He sits down.)

I won't know till tomorrow night about the
crowd from Chelford Castle. They're a bit
over-excited.

                        MOLLY

Why?

                        VERNON

They've got this film company coming to do
a location recce there tomorrow morning.
Very last minute but if they use the castle, the hotel's the best place to put the
crew in. Quids in for the landlord.

                        MOLLY

At last.

                        VERNON

Exactly, so you can imagine, *Hamlet* is a
little lower on his list of priorities. We
could do with his crowd tomorrow night,
mind you. It would swell the coffers.
Anyway I'm still working him over.

                        MOLLY

How?

(CONTINUED)

62 CONTINUED: 62

                         VERNON

          Well, this film is futuristic apparently.
          They are doing the interiors in America
          and cheap locations in Europe. They want
          the castle to be the ruins of an ancient
          city on the planet Zarbok.

                         MOLLY

          Mmmm ... sounds lovely.

                         VERNON

          So I told him to greet the film producer
          in an R2-D2 party hat and a homemade Star
          Trek uniform.

                         MOLLY

          He loves Crimplene.

                         VERNON

          Exactly.

                         MOLLY
                    (she loses her place)
          Oh, flipping heck!
                    (He takes over.)
          Thanks for doing all this Vernon. You've
          been a rock. It's the weirdest Christmas
          holiday from school I've ever spent. Every
          time I think I'm going slightly potty, I
          just look at you ... I mean, nothing seems
          to phase you.

                         VERNON

          Well, it doesn't if you're needed. I like
          being needed. It's a new experience for
          me. I should make a film about it. Being
          needed.

                         MOLLY

          Can I be in it?

                                                       CUT.

63   EXT. PHONE BOX/COUNTRY LANE *and* AGENT'S FLAT
     - LATE AFTERNOON.
                                                                    63

     MARGARETTA is on a treadmill wearing a headpiece telephone
     system and a leotard. She is eating sausages and dipping
     them into tomato ketchup as she exercises in front of the
     television. JOE listening to MARGARETTA, open-mouthed with
     astonishment.

                                                    (CONTINUED)

63 CONTINUED: 63

                              MARGARETTA

          It is astonishing darling ... only Nancy
          Crawford can afford to do it ... of course
          it makes sense in the long run, but it's
          true. They want you for the three pictures
          guaranteed. Guaranteed Joe.

                              JOE

          ... But what if ...

                              MARGARETTA

          They have to pay you darling ... even if
          they don't make the second two ... You get
          more up front but no back end and I'm
          going to fight for a cut of the merchan-
          dising. Of course, we can't hold them for
          ransom if the first picture's a monster
          hit, but we do get three years' money and
          six months a year employment guaranteed,
          in a movie concept that could be Star Wars
          all over again.

                              JOE

          And you're certain Dylan Judd is out of
          the picture?

                              MARGARETTA

          Darling, she has shot herself in the foot,
          the bottom, and most crucially the brain
          ... so greedy ... And remember they still
          had that videotape of your audition from
          all those months ago. They need character
          for these sidekick roles, particularly if
          you're in a suit and latex for all those
          hours.

                              JOE

          Oh my God ... I'm speechless ...

(Telephone pips start.)

          Oh Christ look Mags, I'm going to have to
          run ... Can we talk about this when you
          come down? Look I'll see you at the show
          ... Thanks Mags ...

In his haste he does not replace the receiver properly. We
hear MARGARETTA on the other end of the line.

                              MARGARETTA

                          (panicked)

          ... but Joe, we have to talk, we have to
          talk, start dates, travel arrangements
          ... Joe, Joe.

                                                              CUT.

64   INT. TERRY and HENRY'S BEDROOM - NIGHT.   64

Both in bed miserable. JOE appears at the curtain/wall of
their dorm with two glasses of champagne.

                        JOE
            Peace offering.

He puts the glasses on their bedside table.

                        JOE
            I think you're both fantastic.
                        TERRY
            Naughty girl.
                        HENRY
            Bad person.
                        JOE
            Now you trust me on this make-up issue.
            You'll look great.

He goes. They pick up their champagne.

                        TERRY
            He's right of course, we did look like two
            silly old tarts. We can't make time stand
            still Henry. Those days are gone forever.
                        HENRY
            I suppose so. Fun though wasn't it?
                        TERRY
            Oh yes, it was fun.

                                                        CUT.

65   INT. CARNFORTH/VERNON'S BEDROOM - NIGHT.   65

They are also in bed, CARNFORTH still learning lines. VER-
NON brings in two glasses of champagne. He passes one to
Carnforth.

                        CARNFORTH
            What's all this then?
                        VERNON
            Bribe from the boss.
                        CARNFORTH
            This is very sporting of him.
                        VERNON
            Yes, do you think it's the equivalent of
            Nero fiddling while Rome burned?

                                            (CONTINUED)

65   CONTINUED: 65

                              CARNFORTH
              Oh hardly.

                              VERNON
              Only joking Carnforth. Lighten up.

                              CARNFORTH
              Well, I suppose I would, love, if I didn't
              feel like such an eight billion per cent
              twit.

                              VERNON
              Still having a problem remembering the
              lines are we?

                              CARNFORTH
              The lines, the movement, the costume
              changes, my bloody awful acting, Betty
              Bottle.

                                                           CUT.

66   INT. CHURCH - WEE SMALL HOURS.   66

        FADGE working at one end of the church, painting.
                              TOM
              What are you doing?

                              FADGE
              I'm making an audience.

                              TOM
              I beg your pardon?

                              FADGE
              Well. I've been completely pathetic up to
              now but I think I'm onto something at
              last. If we don't get a natural audience.
              I want to create a World for you. You
              should at least have people watching you.
              Even if they are cardboard.

                              TOM
              That'll be brilliant. They won't cough. I
              hate that.

                                                           CUT.

67   INT. CHURCH - WEE SMALL HOURS.   67

        JOE's office. NINA, MOLLY and JOE carving thick candles and
        fixing them into a great candelabra.

(CONTINUED)

67   CONTINUED: 67

> NINA
>
> Ooo I think that champagne's gone right to
> my head. Is this wise before a first
> night?
>
> JOE
>
> These are unusual circumstances.
>
> MOLLY
>
> Yes, is your bank manager drunk too?
>
> JOE
>
> I think, he was encouraged by some
> Christmas good news, to review my over-
> draft.
>
> MOLLY
>
> What you mean, someone's bought a ticket
> who doesn't know us or he is actually
> drunk?
>
> JOE
>
> All in good time. Let's get the show on
> first before I share the glad tidings.

CUT.

68   INT. CHURCH - WEE SMALL HOURS.   68

FADGE and TOM laugh.

> FADGE
>
> It's good to have a laugh, isn't it?
>
> TOM
>
> Oh yes.
>
> FADGE
>
> On the whole we've got a serious disease.
>
> TOM
>
> I know, I know. But we are being treated
> for it. We did take this job. Fadge, I
> think I could be funny with you.
>
> FADGE
>
> I think you are funny with me. In fact I
> think we're funny with each other. Come
> on, let's get back to being humourless and
> intense. We have an audience to write and
> reviews to make.

(CONTINUED)

68   CONTINUED: 68

     They set about work.

                                                          CUT.

69   INT. CARNFORTH/VERNON'S BEDROOM - NIGHT.   69

                         VERNON
          The problem with you, is it's so easy. It
          drives me mad.

                         CARNFORTH
          Easy? What do you mean easy?

     Beat.

                         VERNON
          I love you.

                         CARNFORTH
          What?

                         VERNON
          I love you.

                         CARNFORTH
          Now Vernon, don't think I'm not flattered,
          it's just ...

                         VERNON
               (laughs)
          No, no as an audience member, I love you.
          As a company member, I love you. As a
          human being, I love you. I can't help it.
          You've got charm, warmth, you're endear-
          ing, you're honest about yourself, about
          your faults, your insecurities. I can't do
          anything about it. I love you and I've
          loved you ever since the first time I saw
          you. The audience can't help themselves
          either, you walk on, they love you.
          Because you're yourself. You're kind and
          vulnerable and ... well ... nice.

                         CARNFORTH
          Do you really think so?

                         VERNON
          I do. But you're so racked with guilt
          about your old Ma's sacrifices, that you
          don't even notice the audience rather
          likes you, or even that you're a very good
          actor.

                                                (CONTINUED)

69 CONTINUED: 69

CARNFORTH thinks.

                        CARNFORTH
            Well ... I ... suppose not. No.
                        VERNON
            So, I wouldn't worry too much about tomor-
            row Carnforth.

                                              CUT.

70 INT. CHURCH - WEE SMALL HOURS.   70
                        NINA
            Well I think I must be off now to
            Bedfordshire.
                   (she goes to the wrong door)
            Wrong way.
                   (nearly walking into a table)
            Oops, nearly. Night.

She exits.

                        MOLLY
            I think you should take her with you.
                        JOE
            Where?
                        MOLLY
            Wherever you go. Wherever.

                                              CUT.

71 EXT. CHURCH. WIDE SHOT - MORNING.   71

FADGE madly pacing, with an armful of books.

                        FADGE
            This is it. Yes, yes. I've got it now,
            that's right. I've got it. I can make a
            decision. Of course, I can, of course I
            can - I can make a decision. That's it,
            got it. Yes, Lord. GO FOR IT.

72 INT. CHURCH - MORNING. (BLACKOUT)   72

Close-up on TOM yelling through the smoke as Fortinbras.

                                              (CONTINUED)

72   CONTINUED: 72

                         TOM
              DARLING, IT IS A NIGHTMARE!

JOE is at the console.

                         JOE
                    (very cheerful)
              Tom, we're fine, we're fine. It's a tech-
              nical - they're always like this. Don't
              worry. We'll go again from the entrance,
              we'll lighten up on the smoke, it'll be
              alright.

TERRY and HENRY are in the wings, observing this.

                         TERRY
              Ooo Martha Moany Guts has changed her tune
              since yesterday, hasn't she?
                         HENRY
              Well he's happy now we all look like TV
              weathermen.

                                                        CUT.

73   INT. CHURCH - LATE AFTERNOON.   73

End of the dress rehearsal. Everyone on stage.

JOE addresses the company.

                         JOE
              Alright, not bad at all. Listen, we were
              nice and relaxed. Technically it was
              remarkably smooth. Fantastic. Well done
              Molly and Nina and everyone who's helping
              out with special effects and moving
              things. That's great.

A noise from the back of the church. JOE turns.

                         MARGARETTA
              Joe, Joe, I'm so glad I've found you.
                         JOE
              Hello Mags ... you're early. We don't go
              up till 7:30 ...

                                                 (CONTINUED)

73 CONTINUED: 73

She rushes up to him.

                         JOE

          Look everyone, this is Margaretta D'arcy,
          my friend, agent and personal investor in
          the show.

                      MARGARETTA
                     (whispering)
          Darling, I've got to talk to you.

                         JOE

          What?

                      MARGARETTA

          Got to talk to you.

                         JOE

          Yeah. OK. Sure. Moll, do the technical
          notes will you ... I'll be with you in two
          minutes. Two minutes.

He goes back to the church doors with MARGARETTA, who imme-
diately engages him in an intense whispered conversation.
We hear MOLLY's notes as we see in close-up NINA's face as
she watches the pair whispering. We see her P.O.V. As MOLLY
finishes, JOE and MARGARETTA come down to the front.

                        MOLLY

          ... so it's up to you Vernon to take off
          the throne before the fight starts, OK?

                        VERNON

          Fine. No problem.

The Company quietens as it is clear JOE has something to
say. They're expecting their last rallying cry for the
first performance. He begins slowly. He seems to be in
shock, tense, uneasy.

                         JOE

          ... I've ... an important announcement to
          make ... after over a year of spectacular
          unemployment during which as I'm sure
          you've all gathered, I've been pretty des-
          perate, I not only have a job, but really
          The Job. Yes ... a guaranteed three pic-
          ture deal in a new science fiction movie
          trilogy ... the bad news ...

MARGARETTA interrupts.

73   CONTINUED: (2)   73

                         MARGARETTA
          I'm sorry, darlings. I'm going to have to
          be the heavy here. The bad news is that
          Joe has to leave tonight.

Shocked silence.

                         MOLLY
          Tonight?

                         MARGARETTA
          Yes, the producer, Nancy Crawford, is in
          the country recce-ing foreign locations.
          She has a private jet leaving Chelford
          Aerodome at 8 o'clock. They start shooting
          interiors in Los Angeles on Boxing Day. It
          couldn't be more last-minute. It's a won-
          derful opportunity for Joe. And there
          really isn't a choice. I'm sure you'll all
          understand but there really is no choice.

Long pause. They are all dumbfounded. Eventually. Slowly.

                         HENRY
          Well ... she's right, Joe ... There is no
          choice ... You've got to go ...

Beat.

                         VERNON
          Congratulations boss. You've saved the
          world from my nose, just in time.

Beat.

                         JOE
          I'm sorry Vernon.

Beat.

                         TOM
          There is no justice and I hate you pas-
          sionately. Go for it, you swine.

Beat.

                         FADGE
          I'm sure you'll get the chance to do it
          again Joe, but just in case, I wanted to
                         (MORE)

                                                      (CONTINUED)

73 CONTINUED: (3)   73

                              FADGE (Cont'd)
          let you know that I had finally cracked
          it.

  The cast starts to leave. Then.

                              NINA
          Don't go. Please don't go.
                              HENRY
          Now come on N -
                              NINA
          He can't ... He mustn't go. Not just for
          us, but for him.
                              TERRY
          Darling there's just no comparison -
                              NINA
          Yes, there is. Two weeks ago we all met up
          to start this adventure and much though we
          didn't care to admit it we were all in our
          various ways depressed, especially you
          Joe. We needed this job, this play, this
          experience. And all through our ups and
          downs and disagreements we've continued to
          need it.
                              JOE
          Yes, we do, Nina, actors do, but the world
          doesn't. Finally it's Shakespeare and
          nobody's interested.
                              NINA
          They're interested in Hope.
                              MARGARETTA
          Look this is all very good and all very
          over-dramatic. But it just isn't fair. You
          can do this bloody play anytime - any-
          where.
                              TOM
          Look, Nina, Joe's only doing what most of
          us would give our right arms to do.
                              JOE
          It means I can pay you all. It can be
          proper.
                              NINA
          It doesn't have to be proper.

(CONTINUED)

73 CONTINUED: (4)   73

                              JOE

          It's Christmas Eve, for Christ sake you
          should all be with your families.

                              NINA

          We're with our family. That's what actors
          do. That's what people do in what's left
          of Hope. They hang on, they stick it out.
          Now, they're here tonight for us and we
          have to do the show for them and if you
          won't do it ... then ... then ...

                              MOLLY

          Then I'll bloody well do it. I'll play
          Hamlet, I practically know it now. It's
          better than cancelling. Everyone knows
          it's a weird production. One more weirdo
          won't make a difference. This is our vil-
          lage. It's our home. We can't let them
          down.

                           MARGARETTA

          Well that's marvellous then isn't it?

Pause.

                              HENRY

          We are all tired and emotional ... you get
          off and catch that plane ... we'd all do
          the same whatever we say now. We're
          actors, we're beggars, that's the way it
          works. We'll do the show tonight with
          young Mistress Molly and we'll drink to
          your health over Christmas dinner tomor-
          row.

TERRY goes to JOE and kisses him on the cheek.

                              TERRY

          Get a suntan.

FADGE goes to JOE to take back his costume.

                              FADGE

          Sorry, Joe.

The rest start moving off. NINA remains on stage
with CARNFORTH. All the others have disappeared backstage.

                              JOE

          Nina ... I ...

                                                        (CONTINUED)

73 CONTINUED: (5)   73

                         NINA

          You put your whole life into this Joe.
          Right from the start. You needed this job.
          You needed it then and you need it now.
          It's not about fame or money or so-called
          wealth and security, it's about nourishing
          your soul, nourishing your heart. And
          that's what you deserve. At the end of the
          day however hard you hug that pay cheque,
          it won't be a person ... it won't be us
          ... it won't be me.

She runs off in tears.

CARNFORTH remains. He and JOE stare at each other.

                       CARNFORTH

          Easy on yourself old chap. I'm afraid we
          can't all afford the luxury of nourishing
          our souls. That's the prerogative of the
          romantics among us, I fear. These things
          happen. What does he say, 'If it be now
          'tis not to come, if it be not to come it
          will be now, if it be not now, yet it will
          come, the readiness is all'.

JOE is left, shell-shocked, with MARGARETTA, who puts an
arm around him and walks him slowly back towards the door
as we

                                                    CUT.

74   INT. BACKSTAGE DRESSING ROOM - NIGHT.   74

NINA pursued by HENRY.

                        HENRY

          Nina. Listen. He's only human. If that had
          been me at his age, I wouldn't even have
          stopped to tell the company. I'd be on my
          way to the airport.

                         NINA

          Yes, but he'd worked so hard.

                        HENRY

          And so have you, which is why you mustn't
          let a beautiful performance like yours be
          spoiled because you're head over heels in
          love.

                                              (CONTINUED)

74   CONTINUED: 74

                         NINA

          Who said I was in love? I just want what's
          best for him. What's best for the company.

                         HENRY

          What's best for the company is if you go
          out there and give the best Ophelia the
          world's ever seen.

                         NINA

          Yes, but he won't be there to see it.

                         HENRY

          D'you think love's about always being in
          the same place at the same time?

                         NINA

          It helps.

                         HENRY

          So is doing your best for your loved one
          wherever they are. It's much harder for
          him than it is for you, if you'll pardon
          my language.

Beat. They hug.

                         HENRY

          What does your Dad say?

                         NINA

          He wasn't in.

                         HENRY

          Well if I was your Dad I'd say, 'Do this
          one for Joe, think of him and the pain
          he's in, and make him proud up there
          in his rather lonely aeroplane.'

She looks at him lovingly.

                         NINA

          You've turned into an old sweetie haven't
          you?

                         HENRY

          No, I'm still a miserable git. And this is
          all a front to stop you from messing up my
          performance.

                         NINA

          Alright, I'll think about it you miserable
          old tart.

They hug.

                                                     (CONTINUED)

74 CONTINUED: (2)   74

                        NINA
          Push off.

                                                    CUT.

75 INT. BACKSTAGE DRESSING ROOM - NIGHT.   75

     MOLLY, now in a state of shock, in front of the mirror,
     being made up by CARNFORTH and TOM. Book in hand, mumbling
     lines to herself incoherently. Starting to shake.

                        TOM
          This is so amazing, Molly, you're actually
          living the actor's nightmare. We all have
          it darling. Dreaming about going on in a
          major role, totally unprepared. It's so
          exciting.

                        MOLLY
          Thanks Tom. Oh God, whoever said actors
          were sissies. I don't know how you do it.
          I feel sick.

                        CARNFORTH
          Don't worry lovely. If I ever forget my
          lines in Shakespeare I always say, 'Crouch
          we here awhile and lurk'. Always seems to
          do the trick.

                        MOLLY
          Why, what happens?

                        CARNFORTH
          Well, nothing normally but, you know, pro-
          vides a moment of intrigue. Gives you a
          chance to think of something or pick up
          the script, maybe.

                        TOM
          The fight! If it all goes wrong, um
          ... drop the sword and take this off and
          throw it at me.

                    (he puts a boot in her right hand)
          Then I say, 'The boot, the boot was poi-
          soned', and die. That should work.

     MOLLY goes green.

                                                    CUT.

77   INT. FRONT OF HOUSE - NIGHT.   77

FADGE is wired. VERNON is putting out the last of the
chairs. People have started to arrive. FADGE tears the
tickets.

                    AUDIENCE MEMBER.

          Hello!

                    FADGE

          Lovely. Anywhere you like. Thank you.
          Would you like a programme?

                    AUDIENCE MEMBER

          Yes please.

                    FADGE

          I'm sorry we don't have any.

She laughs hysterically. The mad-ometer is hitting 11.

                    VERNON
                 (whispering)

          Yes, we do.

                    FADGE
                 (loud)

          Yes, we do.

VERNON passes them to her.

                    VERNON

          That'll be 50p, thank you.

                    FADGE

          That'll be 50p, thank you.

                    AUDIENCE MEMBER

          Any ice-cream?

                    FADGE

          We have herbal teas, natural fruit juice,
          organic rice cakes with balsamic choco-
          late, and ... straw.

                    AUDIENCE MEMBER

          But, any ice-cream?

                    FADGE

          What are you, a fascist?

                    VERNON
                 (whispering again)

          Fadge, I've got the ice-cream. Here in the
          cool box.

                                        (CONTINUED)

77 CONTINUED: 77

                              FADGE
            Vernon, you're a star.
                        (to the audience member)
            Yes, they're here. (Sells them.) Vernon,
            you're a star. I'm completely out of my
            depth here. The paint's still wet on the
            throne, Joe's costume won't fit Molly, the
            smoke machine is probably down at the
            boozer with Carnforth having a quick one
            before the show. If I was any more ner-
            vous, I'd be very very nervous.

                              VERNON
            You're doing wonderfully well, but tell me
            are your nipples hard?

                              FADGE
            If they were any harder, Tom could do
            chin-ups from them.

                                                        CUT.

78 INT. BACKSTAGE DRESSING ROOM - NIGHT.   78

    CARNFORTH kisses TERRY good luck. TOM crosses the screen
    trying to knot his tie ... Manic activity all around him.

                              TOM
            False economy not having a dresser.

                                                        CUT.

79 INT. FRONT OF HOUSE - NIGHT.   79

    A YOUNG MAN sits into shot in the rapidly filling audito-
    rium. FADGE wild in the background. The YOUNG MAN sits qui-
    etly and studies his programme. A distinguished WOMAN in
    middle age sits next to him. A beat, then

                              WOMAN
            My son's in this. Playing about fifteen
            different roles. One of them good we hope.

                              MAN
            Really? My Dad's in it too.

                              WOMAN
            What's he playing?

    A moment.

                                              (CONTINUED)

79 CONTINUED: 79

                              MAN

        I'm not sure.

                                                      CUT.

80   INT. BACKSTAGE DRESSING ROOM - NIGHT.   80

   Off screen we hear FADGE's 'One minute please, one minute
   ladies and gentlemen'. The company waits nervously in the
   wings. MOLLY being helped by NINA and VERNON. Close-ups on
   them all. TERRY holds HENRY's hand and whispers to himself.

                             TERRY

        It is a far, far better thing that I do
        now than I did that night with the sailor
        and the artichoke.

                             HENRY

        Oh hush Mother. Be wonderful.

   Beat. They all look at each other. No more to say. CARN-
   FORTH is the only one who seems rather relaxed.

                           CARNFORTH

                          (cheerily)

        They love me you know.

   The audience starts to hush. The lights are starting to go
   down.

                                                      CUT.

81   INT. AUDITORIUM - NIGHT.   81

   Heads turn as MARGARETTA obsequiously ushers in NANCY CRAW-
   FORD, film producer and undoubted star. She walks down the
   aisle, like ... well ... a star. We track with them. NANCY
   is accompanied by a small entourage, including a man with a
   notebook.

                          MARGARETTA

                         (grovelling)

        That's the beauty of private planes dar-
        ling isn't it? They wait for you. We're
        all so thrilled.

                             NANCY

        Does this guy bother you?

                          MARGARETTA

        No.

81 CONTINUED: 81

                         NANCY
          What is your name?

                         MAN
          Mortimer.

                         NANCY
          He's doing a profile on me for *The London
          Times*. That's a good paper, isn't it?

                         MARGARETTA
          The best.

                         NANCY
          He figured it would be good to cover me
          catching some art.

They sit down. NANCY sits next to one of FADGE's cardboard
people. Nancy looks at him.

                         NANCY
          These are neat. We should take some of
          those and use them when we preview the
          movie.

MARGARETTA laughs. Then smoke covers the pair. The lights
go down. The drum begins.

82 INT. CHURCH - NIGHT.   82

Wide shot of the stage. Enter CARNFORTH through the smoke.
For the first time, it really is rather scary. He moves
slowly, almost in slow-motion then, with great swiftness he
turns round firing a machine gun over the heads of the
audience. The sound is terrifying.

                         CARNFORTH
          'Who's there?'

Great gasps. Close-up of riveted children's faces.

                                                    CUT.

83 INT. CHURCH STAGE - NIGHT.   83

The first Court Scene in progress. HENRY commanding and
good. MOLLY, with her back to the audience is in shadow and

                                              (CONTINUED)

83 CONTINUED: 83

to the side of the stage. The audience can barely see her.
She is aquiver with nerves as the dreaded first line
approaches.

                    HENRY
          ' ... But now, my cousin Hamlet, and my
          son—'

From the back of the auditorium, by the doors, a strong
voice emerges from the gloom.

                    JOE
          'A little more than kin and less than
          kind.'

A little 'Ah' from the audience. Once again they have been
taken by surprise. This is turning out to be rather good.
The scene continues as MOLLY is pulled off the stage. HENRY
and TERRY are clearly delighted, as they instantly adjust
the staging to deal with JOE's new entrance.

                    HENRY
          'How is it that the clouds still hang on
          thee?'

JOE climbs onto the stage.

                    JOE
          'Not so my Lord, I am too much i'th'sun.'

This is too much for TERRY, who, as Gertrude, flings himself, a welter of emotion, at the surprised JOE.

                    TERRY
          'Good Hamlet, cast off thy coloured
          nightie and let thine eye look like a
          friend on Denmark.'

He/she hugs him ferociously as we cut to NANCY CRAWFORD
throwing MARGARETTA a quizzical look in the auditorium. Did
he just say that?

                                        CUT.

84 INT. BACKSTAGE - NIGHT. A LITTLE LATER.   84

TOM beside himself with excitement. From onstage we hear
the sounds of Hamlet and Horatio talking about the ghost.
The others rushing around as ever.

                                        (CONTINUED)

84   CONTINUED: 84

                         TOM

          Darling, darlings, Dorothy Drama has come
          to live with us in a big way. Nancy
          Crawford has delayed her flight to see her
          new boy in action and she's got *The Times*
          with her. We're going to be reviewed dar-
          ling by a national newspaper!

                         NINA

          So he's just come back for the one perfor-
          mance?

                         TOM

          Be reasonable Nina. He's saved the show.
          Saved giving Molly a nervous breakdown and
          saved us the chance of a wonderful notice.

                         NINA

          I think it's shameful.

At that point, the previous scene ends and JOE comes off to
the whispered congrats of CARNFORTH and VERNON. JOE sees
her.

                         JOE

          Nina, I ...

She rushes past, deliberately ignoring him.

                                                         CUT.

85   INT. CHURCH AUDITORIUM - NIGHT.   85

The console. MOLLY, now changed back into normal clothes,
sits down beside FADGE.

                         MOLLY
                    (mock annoyance)
          I was going to be rather good I thought.

                         FADGE
          You knelt beautifully.

She pours a measure of whisky into MOLLY's mug. And takes a
swig herself out of a small bottle of whisky.

Cut.

86   INT. CHURCH - NIGHT.   86

    JOE runs down the centre aisle towards the back doors
    straight to camera.

                          JOE

              'Bloody, bawdy villain!
              Remorseless, treacherous, lecherous, kind-
              less villain!'

87   INT. CHURCH - NIGHT.   87

    FADGE and MOLLY clink glasses.

                                                          CUT.

88   INT. STAGE - NIGHT.   88

    The Nunnery Scene. Playing beautifully. Charged with emo-
    tion. It's the first time JOE and NINA have spoken to each
    other.

                          NINA

              'Good my Lord,
              How does your honour for this many a day?'

                          JOE

              'I humbly thank you, well, well, well'.

                          NINA

              'My lord, I have remembrances of yours
              That I have longed to redeliver.
              I pray you now receive them.'

                          JOE

              'No, not I, I never gave you aught.'

                          NINA

              'My honoured lord, you know right well you
              did,
              And with them words of so sweet breath
              compared
              As made the things more rich. Their per-
              fume lost,
              Take these again, for to the noble mind
              Rich gifts wax poor when givers prove
              unkind.
              There, my lord.'

    With that she gives him an almighty belt around the face.
    The audience gasps.

                                                          CUT.

89   INT. DRESSING ROOM - NIGHT.   89

   NINA storms through the dressing room, past a lot of camp
   raised eyebrows: 'Oooooo'.

                                                   CUT.

90   INT. STAGE - NIGHT.   90

   Later. The play going very well, montage of bits showing
   everyone acting as well as they ever have, utterly real.

                        JOE
              'Madam, how like you this play?'
                        TERRY
              'The lady doth protest too much me
              thinks'.
                        JOE
              'O, but she'll keep her word'.
                        HENRY
              'Have you heard the argument? Is there on
              offence in't?'
                        JOE
              'No, no, they do but jest, poison in jest,
              no offence i'th' world'.
                        HENRY
              'What do you call the play?'
                        JOE
              'The Mousetrap'.

   Uneasy laughter from the court and audience. We feature a
   close-up reaction on TERRY'S SON and CARNFORTH'S MOTHER,
   both rapt.

                                                   CUT.

   The Closet Scene.

                        TERRY
              'What wilt thou do? Thou wilt not murder
              me? Help, help, Ho!'
                        VERNON
              'What ho! Help, help, help!'
                        JOE
              'How now, a rat? Dead, for a ducat, dead.'

                                              (CONTINUED)

90   CONTINUED: 90

JOE thrusts his sword through a sheet, which dramatically
pours blood.

CUT.

                         TERRY
             'Calmly, good Laertes.'

TOM sweaty and butch holding HENRY at sword's length.

                          TOM
                      (savagely)
             'That drop of blood that's calm proclaims
             me bastard.'

Close-up on NANCY CRAWFORD.

                         NANCY
             He's good.

                       MARGARETTA
             He's with me.

                         NANCY
             What's his name?

MARGARETTA hastily looks in the programme.

                       MARGARETTA
             Nina ... NEWMAN, TOM NEWMAN.

CUT.

91   INT. BACKSTAGE - NIGHT.   91

VERNON rushing through, still with his bald cap and sword
through his body, from Polonius's death.

                        VERNON
             ... put the champagne on ice, love. Joe
             will need a bottle on a drip feed directly
             into the vein ... If it had been any
             closer he would have nearly got me ...
             Where's the toilet?

CUT.

92 INT. STAGE - NIGHT.   92

JOE in brilliant form, soliloquizing. Hamlet's pain and
weariness all too clear.

                    JOE
        'What is a man if his chief good and mar-
        ket of his time be but to sleep and feed,
        a beast no more.'

                                                    CUT.

We pan across the excited faces of the audience as we hear
the frightening sounds of the sword fight. Clangs and gasps
and cheers.

                                                    CUT.

Hamlet's Death. A thick silence.

                    JOE
        'The rest is silence.'
                  CARNFORTH
        'Now cracks a noble heart. Good night
        sweet prince.
        And flights of angels sing thee to thy
        rest.'

Close on CARNFORTH'S MUM. Very proud.

                                                    CUT.

93 INT. CHURCH - NIGHT.   93

Close on the audience as we hear Fortinbras's now familiar
line

                    TOM
        'Go, bid the soldiers shoot.'

Darkness. Drum. Gong. Then. Wild applause. The place in an
uproar. Darlings it's a TRIUMPH. We track along the faces
of the company as they take their bows. Ecstatic. FADGE and
MOLLY join the cast to take a bow.

                                                    CUT.

94 INT. BACKSTAGE - NIGHT.   94

Champagne pops, campery erupts, total hysteria.

                        VERNON

        No you were marhvellous daarhling.

                        CARNFORTH

        Noooo, yoou were marvhellous daaarling.

                        VERNON

        No, you were -

                        MOLLY

        Carnforth?

CARNFORTH has stopped camping. His MOTHER has arrived with
MOLLY. CARNFORTH can hardly speak.

                        CARNFORTH

        Mum ... were you? ... did you? ...

                        MRS BRANCH

        I'm afraid I did. And I'm very cross with
        you.

                        CARNFORTH

        Really?

                        MRS BRANCH

        Yes, you broke my heart as Horatio. I was
        in tears most of the evening.

                        CARNFORTH

        Really?

                        MRS BRANCH

        Yes.

                        VERNON

        Would you like a drink Mrs. ...

                        MRS BRANCH

        Yes, please.

FADGE rushes in.

                        FADGE

        It's a triumph. Excuse me, God you were
        good, wasn't he?

                        MRS BRANCH

        Yes.

                        CARNFORTH

        Fadge, our designer.

CUT.

95 INT. DRESSING ROOMS - NIGHT.   95

        TERRY in his place. HENRY enters, with TIM.

                        HENRY
                Terry, visitor for you.
                        TERRY
                Christ.

Pause.

                        TIM
                Hello, Dad. Henry dropped me a line. Told
                me what you were up to.
                        TERRY
                Well, it's not quite *Puss 'n Boots* in
                Bradford is it?
                        TIM
                You were very good in that. I'm sure it's
                just as hard to do panto.
                        TERRY
                Oh, it is love, but a bit easier on the
                heart strings though. How's your ... ?
                        TIM
                She's very well. She sends her best.
                        TERRY
                Really?
                        TIM
                Really. We both got quite a turn from
                Henry's letter. I ... we both thought it
                was time to be a little more ... well, I'm
                just very glad I saw it. I think you're a
                wonderful queen, in every way.
                        TERRY
                Cheeky bugger.

They laugh.

                        TIM
                Look, I'll have to get back Christmas Eve
                and all ... but I'd like to bring Ma
                ... and me girlfriend ... next week maybe?
                ...
                        TERRY
                ... er ... ern ... yes ... lovely.

                                        (CONTINUED)

95   CONTINUED: 95

                         TIM
          Great. Well look. I'll be off. Well done,
          Dad ... I thought you were great.
                         TERRY
          Thank you.

He gives him a hug.

                         TERRY
          Good boy.

TIM leaves.

                         TIM
          Thanks, Harry.
                         HENRY
          HENRY!

TERRY picks up his glass of champagne.

                         TERRY
          Henry Wakefield, what the fuck did you put
          in the letter?
                         HENRY
          I told him you had cholera.

TERRY spits out the drink.

                                              CUT.

97   INT. AUDITORIUM - NIGHT.   97

The audience filing out. NANCY and MARGARETTA talking
intently, stay where they are.

                         NANCY
          ... it's better taller ... taller and
          chunkier, chunky is good ... see I can
          make a lot more value out of the spatial
          relationships.
                         MARGARETTA
          Exactly darling, well you know
          Shakespeare. I mean, if you can get the
          spatial relationships right ... it's
          ...it's ... often can be so much better ...

                                              (CONTINUED)

97   CONTINUED: 97

                              MORTIMER
              I'll go and file this. Editor's rather
              intrigued to have a Shakespeare review in
              panto season. (to Nancy) Thank you.

He goes.

98   INT. DRESSING ROOM - NIGHT.   98

    JOE trying to talk to NINA.
                              JOE
              Look Nina, please let me try to explain.

    NANCY and MARGARETTA approach in the background.
                              NANCY
              Well, if it isn't the very sad Swedish
              person himself.
                              MARGARETTA
              Joe, this is Nancy Crawford.
                              JOE
              Oh. Hello, it was very kind of you to come
              to the play.
                              NANCY
              Listen, I figure I have to check out any
              guy who can turn me down like that. He
              should be worth watching, however stupid.
                              NINA
              You said no ... ?
                              MARGARETTA
              Yes, before the show, rather disproves
              your theory from martyr central, doesn't
              it?

    NINA looks at JOE. Neither knows what to say. TOM and FADGE
    approach from behind them.
                              NANCY
              Still, as in all box-office hits we do
              have a happy ending. I'd like you all to
              meet the new 'Smegma'.

She indicates TOM.
                              TOM
              And my own personal costume designer.

                                                        (CONTINUED)

98 CONTINUED: 98

FADGE beams.

                    NANCY

I loved your little thin people. We're
going to base Smegma's look on some of
these. I mean, it was so neat. The whole
thing was like a Judy Garland movie. (to
Tom) You're gonna be great. I mean, taller
is better. He needs your kind of physique.
And all those different accents. You have
to get lots of character under the latex.
Where are you from originally?

                    TOM

Norway.

                    NANCY

Hey, great for the European investors. Oh
and don't worry honey (to Fadge) I'll make
sure he's naked for the first two weeks of
the shoot, so you have some time for the
costume concept. You're gonna love Nathan,
he's a wonderful designer, he just could-
n't find his Smegma.

                    NINA

Tom, you're playing Smegma in the new Sci-
fi film *Galaxy Terminus*?

                    MARGARETTA

You're too quick for your own good darling.

                    NANCY

Well I hope he is. I don't need any more
fuck-ups on this role. Do you have an
'out' in your contract?

                    TOM

Sorry?

                    NANCY

Did your agent negotiate a way for you to
leave the show, should such a thing happen?

                    VERNON

He doesn't have an agent.

                    MARGARETTA

          (smoothly)

Yes he does, and obviously we'll make some
compensation to the management. We'll talk
about it, Joe.

(CONTINUED)

98   CONTINUED: (2)   98

                                NANCY
            Well, we have a plane to catch ... Bob?

                                TOM
            Tom. I'll be right along.

                                NANCY
            Snatch?

                                FADGE
            Fadge. Right with you boss.

                                NANCY
                    (She starts to go. Turns to Nina and Joe.)
            Mickey and Judy. You two were fine. Keep
            it up kids.

She goes.

                              MARGARETTA
                    (to JOE)
            For what it's worth darling. I thought you
            were a wonderful Hamlet.

She kisses him and starts to go, then stops.
            Do you have representation Snot?

                                FADGE
            Fadge.

                              NANCY O/S
            Margaretta!

MARGARETTA rushes out.

                              MARGARETTA
            Coming Nancy.
                    (she hands Fadge her card)
            Here, call me.

They are gone. All the actors are now gathered.

                                TOM
            I think I'm going to faint.

                                FADGE
            Oh, God Joe it's alright isn't it? I mean
            my work's done here and Molly can just as
            easily fill in for Tom, can't she?

(CONTINUED)

98   CONTINUED: (3)   98

                              JOE
          Of course, it's alright Fadge, and with
          the compensation we can hire someone to
          work the lights and sell the tickets. It's
          alright. I'm delighted for you both.
          Really I am.

                              ALL
          We all are, etc.

                              TERRY
          This whole Christmas is like a fairy tale.

                              HENRY
          Bloody nightmare more like.

                              TERRY
          Shut up.

                              CARNFORTH
          Oh Nina darling, just remembered there's a
          visitor for you out front.

                              ALL
          Oooo!

                                                          CUT.

99   INT. CHURCH - NIGHT.   99

     Empty auditorium save one man. All the actors come out
     after NINA, who stops a moment, peering into the semidark-
     ness.

                              NINA
          ... Dad ... ? DAD!

     She runs towards him, tripping, of course, at the last bit
     and falling into his arms.

                              NINA
          I can't believe it, I can't believe you
          came, did you like it, did you?

                              DAD
          You were wonderful.

     She turns, the whole company are on the stage, drinks and
     party gear in hand. JOE at the front.

99 CONTINUED: 99

                          NINA

          Oh, Dad, this is my family. I mean my
          friends, they're all wonderful, I mean
          you'll meet them all, and this is
          ... (indicating Joe) the most utterly ...

                          JOE

          Stupid ...

                          NINA

          Heroic man.

She runs to him. Hugs him. The company watches. Her Dad
watches. This conversation is just for the two of them and
all of them.

                          NINA

          I'm so proud of you.

                          JOE

          Thank you, it isn't often you turn down
          life-long financial security and a great
          career.

                          NINA

          Rubbish. You have a great career. And you
          have me.

                          JOE

          Really?

                          NINA

          If you'd like.

                          HENRY

          Get his name on the dotted line love. He's
          a shifty git.

VERNON switches the music on.

                          NINA

          Would you like to dance?

                          JOE

          I thought you didn't dance?

                          NINA

          I thought better of it
                    (they start to dance slowly)
          and I reckon if I play my cards right I
          might get my leg over tonight.

                                                          (CONTINUED)

99   CONTINUED: (2)   99

> JOE
>
> I'm not just a fabulously attractive sex
> object you know.
>
> NINA
>
> Yes you are.
>
> JOE
>
> Fair enough. Won't your Dad be rather
> appalled at this?
>
> NINA
>
> Oh he knows all about you. Check out his
> phone bill. I think he's just accepted his
> last reverse charge call from me.

Around them everyone's starting to dance. TOM with FADGE,
MOLLY with VERNON, HENRY with TERRY, and CARNFORTH, a bit
pissed, with NINA's DAD.

> CARNFORTH
>
> Actors: they're all the same aren't they?
>
> DAD
>
> This is marvellous.
>
> JOE
>
> You know, despite my immense purity of
> soul and being cleansed by my art, I'm
> still always going to get depressed and
> mad.
>
> NINA
>
> Well we can get depressed together, that's
> fun.
>
> JOE
>
> Are you always going to be optimistic?
>
> NINA
>
> No, I'm going to be miserable and fat and
> get a huge saggy ass.
>
> JOE
>
> Mmmm lovely. I can just feel it starting
> actually ...

CUT.

100   EXT. CHURCH - NIGHT.   100

The midnight bell strikes.

(CONTINUED)

100   CONTINUED: 100

> NINA O/S
>
> Listen everyone, Merry Christmas.
>
> ALL O/S
>
> Merry Christmas!

We fade to BLACK. As the credits start, a beautiful rendition of the hymn 'In The Bleak Midwinter' begins.

The end.

Above: *'Dylan Judd…? But he's… he's… he's short.' Joe (Michael Maloney) dealing with his reaction to a successful rival. Margaretta (Joan Collins) is amused.*

STILLS

Above: *Joe (Michael Maloney) expresses his frustration at the rival.*

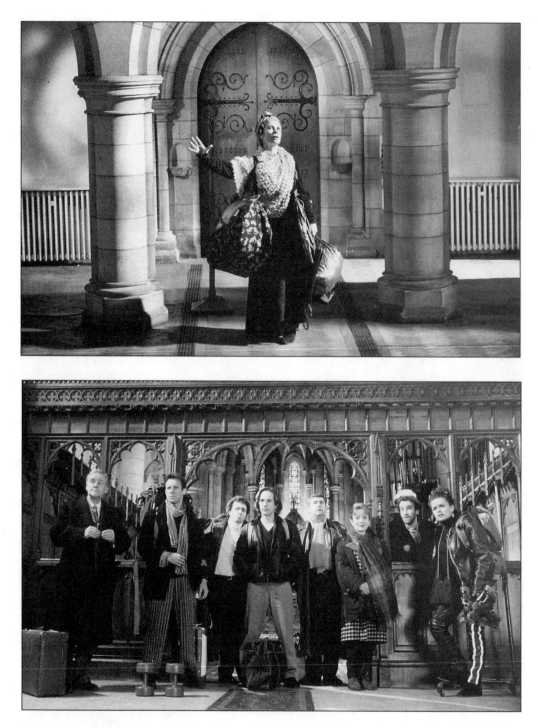

Top: *'I feel something very powerful and strange.' Fadge (Celia Imrie) taking in the atmosphere of the church.*

Bottom: *The company comes face to face with their remarkable designer.*

Top: *'You won't fail,' says Nina (Julia Sawalha). Joe (Michael Maloney) is not so sure.*
Bottom and right: *The company 'warm-up'.*

Top: 'Can I just mention smoking?' Tom (Nicholas Farrell) makes an unpopular remark to a nervous company at the start of the read-thru.

Bottom: The company observing Tom's request.

Opposite page, left: Terry's Gertrude (John Sessions) in a moment of feminine harmony with Nina's Ophelia (Julia Sawalha).

Top: *'It's a bit limp.' Joe (Michael Maloney) inspires Carnforth (Gerard Horan) to produce fear as Bernardo.*

Bottom: *Carnforth (Gerard Horan) considers the crossword that he will always complete, regardless of the right answers.*

Top: 'Do you intend anyone to come and see this boss?' enquires Vernon (Mark Hadfield). Molly (Hetta Charnley) muses over the box office charts.

Bottom, Left: 'To be or not to be?' Joe (Michael Maloney) muses on his fate as Hamlet and as a director.

Bottom, Right: 'It's Christmas darling, why don't you write to Santa?' Joe receives advice from Margaretta (Joan Collins).

Top: *Tom (Nicholas Farrell) and Carnforth (Gerard Horan) in soldierly form as Fortinbras and his slightly tipsy Captain.*

Bottom: *'Not bad, eh love?' Henry (Richard Briers) and Terry (John Sessions) reveal their 'look'. Nina (Julia Sawalha) and Vernon (Mark Hadfield) say nothing.*

Opposite Page: *Joe (Michael Maloney) and Molly (Hetta Charnley) react to the intriguing makeup ideas provided by Terry and Henry.*

Top: *'I have some good news and some bad news.' Joe (Michael Maloney) prepares the company for his departure. Margaretta (Joan Collins) looks on.*

Bottom: *The company reacts to this fresh hell.*

Top: *'Vernon, you're a star.' Fadge (Celia Imrie) is rescued at the last minute by an ice-cream laden Vernon (Mark Hadfield).*

Bottom: *'I promise it will be marvellous dahling.' A nervous Margaretta (Joan Collins) persuades Nancy (Jennifer Saunders).*

Top: *Nina (Julia Sawalha) takes her revenge on Joe (Michael Maloney) in a very heartfelt performance.*
Bottom: *'Give me my father.' Tom (Nicholas Farrell) gives us his Laertes to Henry's (Richard Briers)*
   Claudius.

131

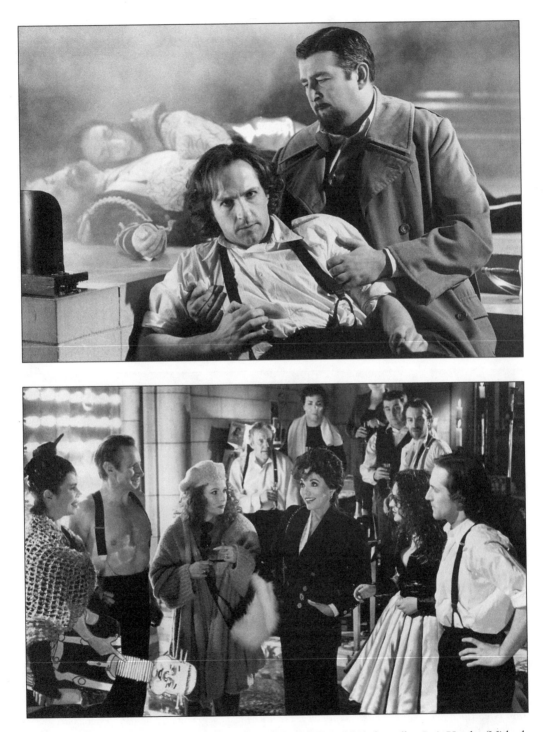

Top: *'Good night, sweet prince.' Carnforth's Horatio (Gerard Horan) bids farewell to Joe's Hamlet (Michael Maloney).*

Bottom: *Nancy (Jennifer Saunders) finds her Smegma. And Tom (Nicholas Farrell) finds a new agent.*

CAST AND CREW CREDITS

CASTLE ROCK ENTERTAINMENT Presents
A Midwinter Films Production
A Kenneth Branagh Film

A MIDWINTER'S TALE

Starring in Alphabetical Order

Richard Briers	Gerard Horan
Hetta Charnley	Celia Imrie
Joan Collins	Michael Maloney
Nick Farrell	Julia Sawalha
Mark Hadfield	John Sessions

With

Jennifer Saunders
Ann Davies
Robert Hines
James D. White

Original Music by Jimmy Yuill
Costume Designer – Caroline Harris
Editor – Neil Farrell
Director of Photography – Roger Lanser
Production Designer – Tim Harvey
Associate Producers – Iona Price and Tamar Thomas
Produced by David Barron
Written and Directed by Kenneth Branagh

Henry	Richard Briers	Audience Member	Carol Starks
Molly	Hetta Charnley	Nina's Father	Edward Jewesbury
Margaretta	Joan Collins	Assistant Director	Simon Moseley
Tom	Nicholas Farrell	Camera Operator	Trevor Coop
Vernon	Mark Hadfield	Sound Mixer	Peter Glossop
Carnforth	Gerard Horan	Script Supervisor	Anna Worley
Fadge	Celia Imrie	Chief Makeup/Hair	Jenny Shircore
Joe	Michael Maloney	Property Buyer	Celia Bobak
Nancy Crawford	Jennifer Saunders	2nd Assistant Director	Emma Pounds
Nina	Julia Sawalha	Gaffer Electrician	Ken Pettigrew
Terry	John Sessions	Location Manager	Tom White
Mrs. Branch	Ann Davies	Production Accountant	John Sargent
Tim	James D. White	1st Assistant Editor	Daniel Farrell
Mortimer	Robert Hines	2nd Assistant Editor	Robbie Broughton
Tap Dancer	Allie Byrne	Sound Editor	Richard Fettes
Young Actor	Adrian Scarborough	Assistant Sound Editor	Melanie Viner Cuneo
Ventriloquist	Brian Petifer	Focus Pullers	Nick Penn
Scotsman	Patrick Doyle		Simon Finney
Mule Train Man	Shaun Prendergast	Clapper Loader	Skip Margetts

Grip	Darren Quinn
Camera Trainee	Marc Atherfold
Grips Assistant	Michael Cuming
Boom Operator	Clive Fleury
Sound Assistant	Tom Glossop
Re-Recording Mixers	Robin O'Donoghue
	Dominic Lester
Re-Recording Facility	Twickenham Film Studios
Foley Recorded by	Delta Sound Services
Foley Mixer	Ed Colyer
Foley Editor	Gerard McCann
Dialogue Editor	Jim Roddan
Assistant Dialogue Editor	Kevin Ahern
Editing Trainee	Jens Baylis
Music Recorded at	Air Edel Recording Studios
Music Engineers	Paul Hulme
	Tom Meadows
Makeup Artists	Ivana Primorac
	Christine Whitney
Miss Saunders Makeup	Joan Hills
Miss Collins Hair	Sally Harrison
Wardrobe Mistress	Caroline Kelly
Wardrobe Assistants	Claire Porter
	Geraldine Geraghty
Miss Collins Costumes by	Nicole Farhi
Miss Saunders Costumes by	Betty Jackson
Assistant Art Director	Nic Pallace
Prop Master	Frank Billington Marks
Standby Props	Peter Grant
Best Boy Electrician	Billy Merrell
Electricians	Tom O'Sullivan
	John Curtis
Fight Arranger	Nick Hall
Stunts	Chrissie Monk
Skating Coach	Nola Haynes
3rd Assistant Directors	Matthew Penry-Davey
	Emma Griffiths
Production Assistants	Sally Ross
	Rebecca Ciallella
Stagehand	Michael Cohen
Painter	Peter Mounsey
Riggers	Alf Newvell
	Ian Rolfe
Publicity	Corbette and Keene
Stills	David Appleby
Transport Captain	Terry Pritchard
Unit Drivers	Mike Bevan
	Paul Gamby
Title Design	Simon Giles
	Alan Church
Payroll Services	Sargent Disc Ltd.
Fire Protection	Sec Fire and Rescue Ltd.
Health and Safety	Brian Shemmings
Unit Nurse	Anne Casey
Catering Services by First Choice Location Services	
Location Transport	D & D International Ltd.

Facilities	Location Facilities Ltd.
Lighting Equipment	Lee Lighting Ltd.
Processing and Prints	Rank Film Laboratories Ltd.
Laboratory Supervisor	Ray Adams
Opticals	The Magic Camera Company
Editing Equipment	Edit Hire Ltd.

Lenses and Panaflex Camera by
Panavision ®
Originated on Eastman Film from Kodak
Spectral Recording ®
Dolby Stereo Digital
Verify Theatre Format

"Why Must the Show Go On"
Written by Noël Coward © Chappell Music Ltd
by kind permission of Warner Chappell Music Ltd.
Recording Courtesy of Sony Classical
by Arrangement with Sony Music
Entertainment (UK) Ltd.
Performers cleared by American
Federation of Musicians

"In the Bleak Midwinter"
(Gustav Holst)
Arranged by Jimmy Yuill

"Mule Train"
(Lange, Heath, Glickman)
Copyright © 1949 Bulls Eye Music Inc. USA
Used by permission of
Campbell Connelly & Co. Ltd. London

"Heart of Glass" (Deborah Harry & Chris Stein)
Published by Chrysalis Music Inc.

With Special Thanks to Michael Redding, Danny
Hunter, Angels and Bermans, Julian MacCloud, Phil
Turner, Paul Olliver, Denis Carrigan, Ron Pearce,
Hugh Whittaker, Peter MacCrimmon, Robin
O'Donoghue, Gerry Humphries, Dennis Bartlett,
Peter Gundry, Ben Elton, Special Treats, Billy
Hinshelwood, Maggie Rodford, Michael J. Smith,
Richard Bonneville, Shaun Webb, & The Picture
Production Company.

Filmed on Location and at Shepperton Studios,
Shepperton, London, England.

Copyright © 1995 Midwinter Films Ltd.
All Rights Reserved

Midwinter Films is the author of this film/motion
picture for the purpose of copyright and other laws.

The persons and events portrayed in this production
are ficticious. No similarity to actual persons, living
or dead, is intended or should be inferred.